S0-ASL-475

Praise for *Candy* by Luke Davies

"Beautifully written and tear-provokingly poignant."
—*The Daily Telegraph*

"The writing is lean and strong . . . affable characters."
—*Booklist*

"Hard to put down."   —*Kirkus Reviews*

"Luke Davies expertly maps the constricted corridor of love and addiction in *Candy*. . . . It's a stunning novel, compassionate and knowingly observed."   —Barry Lopez

"Strong . . . harrowing."   —*Publishers Weekly*

Also by Luke Davies

Isabelle THE Navigator

LUKE DAVIES

𝓑

BERKLEY BOOKS, NEW YORK

$\mathcal{B}$

A Berkley Book
Published by The Berkley Publishing Group
A division of Penguin Putnam Inc.
375 Hudson Street
New York, New York 10014

This is a work of fiction. Names, characters, places, and incidents either
are the product of the author's imagination or are used fictitiously, and any
resemblance to actual persons, living or dead, business establishments, events, or
locales is entirely coincidental.

Copyright © 2000 by Luke Davies
Book design by Simon Paterson
Cover illustration by Kamil Voljnar

All rights reserved.
This book, or parts thereof, may not be reproduced in any form without
permission.
BERKLEY and the "B" design are trademarks belonging to Penguin Putnam Inc.

PRINTING HISTORY
Originally published in 2000 by Allen & Unwin, Australia
Berkley trade paperback edition / September 2002

Visit our website at
www.penguinputnam.com

Library of Congress Cataloging-in-Publication Data

Davies, Luke, 1962–
Isabelle the navigator / Luke Davies
p. cm
ISBN 0-425-18604-0
1. Young women—fiction.   2. Fathers—Death—Fiction.   3. Australians—
France—Fiction.   4. Loss (Psychology)—Fiction.   5. Paris (France)—Fiction.
6. Australia—Fiction.   I. Title.

PR9619.3.D29 I8 2002
823'.914—dc21   2002022826

PRINTED IN THE UNITED STATES OF AMERICA

10   9   8   7   6   5   4   3   2   1

To Karen Brien, fearless explorer

We must, incidentally, make it clear from the
beginning that if a thing is not a science, it is not
necessarily bad. For example, love is not a science.

RICHARD P FEYNMAN
*Six Easy Pieces: The Fundamentals
of Physics Explained*

Isabelle THE
Navigator

Luke Davies

PROLOGUE

The Funeral

Around the time my father died was around the time I discovered the sheer poetry of the Beaufort Scale, that extraordinarily concise chart for mariners that relates wind forces to sea states. I was adrift in Paris for a year or two after Matt had died, and one day found the Scale hanging on the back wall of an old bookshop. Studying it, I realised that everything, the whole of life, is just like a series of sea states. The very concept of solid ground is a myth. The galaxy itself is adrift. Then in 1999 I turned thirty and my father died at fifty-six and I came back from Paris for his funeral. Dad had been losing his mind for quite some time. Yet his death could hardly be called a relief. At the funeral I began to cry, not so much for what had been, but for what might have been. He might have been happy. I cried for months.

When you talk about love, and family, invariably too you are talking about compassion. This would include the notion that we are all just lumped together, and tolerance is a virtue.

The ocean, though, is liable to remind us that things are very small, that memory has its limits and that even thirty years is a long and weary stretch. What passes relentlessly through the years is blood, and time; all the bitterness or warmth along the way is almost incidental. Even blood gets forgotten eventually, bleached into stories which are bleached into myth which are bleached of all colour into ashes of myth.

Nothing should come as a surprise and yet everything is astonishing. Out of the oceans the continents form. Then everything moves forward and there are only the rarest of paths back to mute rest, as in madness, as in my father, and the way he died. I have no idea what it all comes to mean, in the end. What everyone fails to notice, when talking to the other humans, to mothers and lovers and strangers in the street, is the one obvious point: 'future corpse, future corpse.'

When the pallbearers lifted his coffin so effortlessly onto their shoulders, a wrenching anguish tore at my heart and I began to sob with that oxygen-depleted heaving felt in deep dreams. Over many years I'd watched Dad, lanky giant though he was, grow smaller, a shrinkage that seemed to signal not just the bones becoming brittle, but the soul's attempt to condense those bones in preparation for an easier return to dust; the soul's preparations for discarding, in some bizarre physics brought on by death's approach, the ballast that would hold back its own sudden soaring into vertiginous realms beyond atmosphere. But maybe it was just a trick of perspective, his receding from us all.

What was acute that day was my awareness of the imminent absence of his actual body from my life and the planet. A terrifying sense of his insubstantiality consumed me; at the same time it was almost comic, the pallbearers like poker-faced muscle men hoisting shoulderwards a balsawood coffin. It seemed to me suddenly that we live half our lives and then watch ourselves wither. It's an awful state of affairs. There was no more future between Dad and me, only a series of moments of connection in the past. Everything was now contained in my mind.

Late at night, the night of the funeral, after the wake when everybody got drunk, I dreamt, in that heady mixture of grief and the glimpse funerals give us into our own impending doom, that the funeral was happening all over again. The only difference was that the interment took place on swampy ground, a kind of mossy sponge across which the funeral party bounced like the *Apollo* astronauts on the moon.

In the dream I began to cry, profusely, just as I had in reality earlier in the day. My crying woke me up and seamlessly continued. It was 4 a.m. I sobbed myself into calmness. A while later I fell back to sleep.

I woke again just before dawn. In Sydney the day always starts white, then the light turns pale yellow before darkening gradually into the greeny-blue of morning. Later the day bakes out into a blue so rich and hard that its echo, its glare, is white. And then evening comes to soften everything, dark blue flaring into mauve after sunset, and the glide into dark red and darkness. Tom Airly was dead. My mother's tragedy, and mine. In a hundred years' time it would be no-one's. I snuggled into the sheets and looked around the walls of my bedroom. They were simply too white.

In the days that followed I painted with meticulous care, on one of the walls, the Beaufort Scale. Admiral Sir Francis Beaufort had died one hundred and fifty years earlier, and here he was, this beautiful man (as I imagined him) invading my room with the lucidity of his language. Notable for its beauty as well as its brevity and practicality, this two-page chart was still the world standard, the common navigational language for describing the force of winds and storms. I loved the lunacy of the notion of trying to structure, with small words, the forces of the weather.

My mother, Tess, thought me moderately unhinged, but pretty much any behaviour is excusable after the dislocation of death. I photocopied the chart onto a transparency; borrowed from a teacher friend an overhead projector; projected the image onto the long white wall of my bedroom; and traced from that a faint stencil. Even the enlarged letters looked beautiful: the curves and serifs, the commas, the slither of the s and the hoops of the g. Slowly, meticulously, I painted black in the stencil, and the chart emerged.

And the fact that my father was gone was made somehow easier to bear in the months that followed by the presence of the words on my wall. In the slow haze of waking I would let my eyes wander over the lissom phrases all around me. Across the top of the wall, near the ceiling, was written, in the largest capitals, **BEAUFORT WIND SCALE**, and beside that, in smaller capitals, WITH CORRESPONDING SEA STATE CODES. The chart was divided vertically into eight columns, five of which were filled with technical details and terminologies, and three of which contained the poetry.

There were thirteen ways, according to Beaufort, in which the wind could be described as affecting the oceans and the planet. Force Zero was an almost non-existent wind, less than a knot, and Force 12 was a hurricane. One read across the columns 'Effects observed far from land,' 'Effects observed near coast' and 'Effects observed on land,' and could guess the corresponding wind speed and Beaufort number. Or one could, like me, read the chart for pleasure, and as a way of defining one's future.

Sometimes when I closed my eyes I could sense my life as a movement through ocean. The past recedes from view until finally it disappears, and all that is properly visible is our most recent wake, which is foam, a bobbing chaos where it was easy for a while to live. Everything converges into a point ploughing into the future. And the future, while it gives the illusion of unfolding, is always just beyond the approaching horizon. I was thirty years old—have I said that? My mother was a woman whose present consisted of the echo of old events. My uncle Dan, though I loved him still, was taboo. My father was dead by his own hand, and anyway had been crazy for years, ever since he came out of prison. Matt had gone under the wheels of a truck two years earlier. It's an old, old world. But I would lie in bed looking at the Beaufort wall and the day would begin to take on colour.

My eyes would roam over the wall: 'far from land.' I pictured the different workings of the wind. *Sea like mirror.* I imagined the wind beginning, the faintest breath, like a lover's exhalation on the back of the ear. *Ripples with appearance of scales; no foam crests... Small wavelets; crests of glassy appearance, not breaking.* And then the *crests begin to break* and there are *scattered whitecaps* and later *numerous whitecaps* gathering on the ocean in my mind.

I loved the transition from 'strong breeze' to 'near gale': it seemed so sudden. *Sea heaps up; white foam from breaking waves begins to be blown in streaks.* And now the *edges of crests begin to break into spindrift,* and the *sea begins to roll* and there are *dense streaks of foam*—my eyes were wide open, sailing all over the beautiful Beaufort wall, and yet it's as if the whole room was filled with television static—and there are *very high waves with overhanging crests* and the *rolling is heavy* now, and I am feeling heavy. *Air filled with foam; sea completely white with driving spray; visibility greatly reduced.* It was as if a wave rolled over me.

My eyes came at last to 'Effects observed on land.' Being the most recognisable to me, these descriptions were somehow the most beautiful. When the sea is like a mirror far from land, the day here on shore is *calm; smoke rises vertically.* Soon the wind is *felt on face; leaves rustle; vanes begin to move.* It's like those early scenes in *The Wizard of Oz: leaves, small twigs in motion; light flags extended.* The day is broiling upwards. The excitation of molecules. *Dust, leaves and loose paper raised up; small branches move.* Force 5, *small trees in leaf begin to sway,* and soon there are *larger branches of trees in motion* and *whistling heard in wires.* Then it's *whole trees in motion,* and I pictured their shimmying, their whiplash. *Resistance felt in walking against wind.*

It gets worse. I mean better. Wilder. *Twigs and small branches broken off trees; progress generally impeded. Slate blown from roofs.* And then Force 10: *seldom experienced on land; trees broken or uprooted; considerable structural damage occurs.* And at last, the strangely unspecific but ominous Force 12: *very rarely experienced on land; usually accompanied by widespread damage.* I slept again and dreamt of giant waves.

On such a morning, a few weeks after the paint had dried, with a hard blue sky forming outside the windows, I woke and felt the need for less dreamy forms of action. There would be time for a swim before I went to the TAFE college to enrol in marine-navigation night classes, a decision I had made, surprisingly enough, in Paris, along with the decision to learn to scuba dive. It's not that I intended to make a life at sea, nor would I have known how to go about that. It's just that you reach a point where metaphors become indistinguishable from the things they represent. And the life you ought to be living is the one you *are* living. And it feels like being born. I only knew that a life *as if* at sea was possible, the rolling grace of movement. We are all, without knowing it, straining at our moorings. The dock creaks. The planet spins endlessly on its axis. The wind sweeps over us. Beyond the horizon all certainty tumbles away; we would love to make that place our home.

PART

One

Every lover loves, first and foremost, an absentee. Absence precedes presence, in the hierarchical order of things. Presence is just a special case in the category of absence. Presence is a hallucination protracted for a certain period. But this in no way diminishes our pain.

ROBERTO CALASSO
Ka: Stories of the Mind and Gods of India

Tess and Tom

WHEN MY FATHER, TOM AIRLY, STARTED SEEING MY mother, Tess, he was nineteen and she was sixteen, about to finish school, about to start training as a nurse. This was a happy coincidence, since Tom was in his second year of medicine—a fact that went some way towards negating Tess's mother's disapproval. He had done so well at school that he'd won a scholarship to the University of Sydney.

Grandmother Constance, despite her own father, George, working in the steelworks, always felt that Tess had married a little 'beneath her station,' because the Airly boys came from Petersham and had gone to the local state schools. 'Can't trust that pair,' she said in various permutations over the years. On the day Tom went to the volcano I have no doubt she would have felt this to be, had she been alive, the ultimate vindication of her belief. In the meantime, for most of the 1960s and seventies and into the eighties, nursing and stroking her own bitterness like a favourite cat, she brooded about her own husband, John Carter, who had simply vanished in 1946, when Tess was born.

Sometimes the three of them would go out together, Tom and Tess and Tom's younger brother, Dan, my uncle, who was eighteen. Mum found it hard to believe they were actually brothers, though in the shape of the nose and the lips she could see it was true. Tom was tall and almost spindly, with the red hair and green eyes that I would inherit. Dan was shorter and stronger, with brown eyes that seemed black, and dark hair swept back with Brylcreem. When I was a very young girl, the smell of Uncle Dan's hair when I ran to hug him would make me think of the olden times, the place from which Dan had emerged fully formed—the 1950s, or the distant, early sixties—a kind of film set that existed outside the known universe. The smell, and his thick tattoo, the faded blue of the mermaid on his forearm.

Tess loved Tom because, above all, he was so gentle. All she really knew of her own father came from the picture Constance painted, some fugitive quality, the absence that surrounded him as if he were no more than a hole in the atmosphere; the cold-bloodedness of his desertion.

Tess loved those early dates with Tom. Her whole teenage life had been lived in the shadow of her mother's dourness. The world was a place not to be trusted; Constance's hatred knew no apparent earthly bounds. So the boys were like the messengers of light. Tom, aloof and gawky, was unbearably handsome to Tess, his very flame-red hair a portent of release from a childhood of darkness.

The three went to the drive-in movies. Tess felt a sharp pang of delight at the extravagant amount of sweets and popcorn the boys bought. They sat three abreast in the front seat of the old Holden and saw *Jason and the Argonauts*. Tess leaned into Tom's chest and he stroked her hair softly. They squealed in mock-terror when the harpies descended upon the blind Phineas among the ruined pillars, or during the battle with the Cyclops or—her favourite part—when the skeletons gathered themselves up from the ground and fought Jason and his men on the edge of the cliff.

Nothing is invented here: you have to believe, I cross-referenced all my stories, extracting the last bit of detail like water squeezed from a towel. From Tess to Dan, and while he was alive and making sense, Tom himself.

They went on a picnic to Palm Beach. This is 1964, maybe '65. Tess invited Elaine along, a friend from her nursing class, in an effort to match Elaine and Dan, and of course the match worked, but of course not for long. Tumbling together in the surf, Tess's hand suddenly and accidentally brushed against the bulge in Uncle Dan's swimming trunks. A shiver ran through her and she erased the event from her mind. Perhaps I have entirely made that part up. But something had to happen, somewhere. There had to be a starting point. Later, in the park behind the beach, the four of them set up a picnic blanket beneath the shade of a huge Moreton Bay fig. They ate cheese and drank Resch's Dinner Ale kept cool in the esky. I imagine the radio playing the latest hit from the Shadows.

Tom told funny stories from his med school class, his voice dry and laconic as he did the character impersonations, Tess and Dan and Elaine rolling about, laughing.

It came as a surprise to my mother, Tess Carter, that falling in love could happen so smoothly and easily.

The fragments that she knew about her mother and father—the dress shop in Newcastle, the handsome John Carter in uniform and off to war—didn't lend themselves easily to the notion of falling in love, that sensation of gliding and irreversible momentum, that fall from a height, when all things change. Perhaps there were many missing pieces in Constance's story. Perhaps there had been passion in the heart of that seventeen-year-old girl. But it was all so long ago—the Second World War—and it was hard for Tess to imagine Constance as anything other than her bitter mother, a core sucked of juice and spat out by life, prematurely grey in body and spirit.

The most my mother could imagine was that a courtship had occurred. Courtship was the word that worked. John Carter courted Constance Hapgood in his breaks from the war, on leave. People in the war didn't fall in love. But in 1965 the world was different and Tess Carter was falling in love with Tom Airly. In 1965 the world was new and clean. Love, too, was a modern thing.

The love affair drifted onwards through the sweet-smelling seasons. In 1966 Tom proposed, and with heart overflowing, Tess said yes. Yes I will take my due. Yes we will grow young forever. In 1968, after Tom's first full year as an intern, they married. Emerging from the vestibule of the Immaculate Conception Church, Tess saw the grains of rice and the blossoms rain down in slow motion from out of a cloudless sky as if the sumptuousness of all love and life were compressed into those seeds and flowers arcing gracefully to earth.

To prove it, I was born in 1969.

Meat Truck

'LOOK, A DRAGONFLY!'

'Dragonfly?'

I pointed to the insect on the inside of the windshield.

'That's a ladybird, darling. A lady beetle.'

'Oh.'

We drove through the afternoon traffic. I watched the bug's progress across the glass.

'You know, once upon a time—this is a long, long time ago—all the animals were very big. Even the insects, like this one.'

'How big?'

'Maybe... I think there were dragonflies as big as this van. There were beetles as big as Volkswagens. See that Volkswagen there? That's called a Beetle. They named it after beetles just like this lady beetle. Only bigger.'

'Was this before I was born, Uncle Dan?'

'Sweetheart, it was even before *I* was born. I guess this was the time of the dinosaurs.'

He is still a mystery to me. It's all a mystery. And yet I loved him almost as much as my father. When I was young Tom spent many years building up his surgery, a small suburban practice, and though we passed long hours together in the evenings, at times in my growing-up I was more familiar with Uncle Dan's company. This was due not so much to the amount of time we spent together—it was not, in actual fact, a great deal—but to the intense pleasure I gained from exploring the world from the cabin of the meat truck. On certain days, when I was four or five years old, in the years before school began, Uncle Dan would take me with him on the meat run.

On such days I felt special; the air would glow with possibility, the frenzy of traffic promised new adventures. Our conversations rambled everywhere. Since parents are merely everything, Dan was like the first separate adult I ever knew.

'Uncle Dan?'

'Sweetie?'

'When I grow up I'm going to buy an island and make it my own country, and there'll only be three laws.'

'Your own country. That sounds terrific.'

'Do you want to know the laws?'

'Tell me the laws.'

'Firstly, everybody has to dance.'

'I'd be into that! What, dance all the time?'

'No, of course not. But every day, at least. At least one time. Secondly, the killing of animals. If you kill an animal you have to do five days' work in the animal hospital.'

'That sounds okay. What's the third law?'

'Um, no cutting of trees. If you cut down a tree you have to plant a new one.'

'Sounds like a beautiful place to me. Does it have a name?'

'It's called Marine Island. And the people are called Marinelles.'

'And you'll be the queen.'

'No, there's no need for a queen, silly. I'll just be one of the people who live there.'

'Can I live there?'

'Of course you can.'

'Okay. Well, we'd better make this a fruit and vegetable truck, then.'

'And in the backyard I'll have a rabbit.'

Whereas my dad kept the family car clean, vacuumed it at least every other weekend, and regularly replaced the plastic deodoriser adhered to the dash, Uncle Dan's meat van seemed to me a fundamental thing of earthiness. No effort was ever made to clean the cabin, which had become a repository for all the small things that passed through

Dan's working life, accreting layers in an archaeological fashion: empty biros, chip wrappers, petrol receipts, soft drink cans, blinker-light fuses, coins, crushed matchboxes. The cabin smelt of engine grease and hamburgers, though the dominant odour was what emanated from the cavernous refrigerated van itself: the raw sweet smell of carcass blood and sawdust.

In the rubble behind the driver's seat Uncle Dan kept three old phone books. I would sit on these and he would clip me into my seat belt and the day would be mine, like a movie, an exciting melee of traffic and colour and diesel fumes.

I loved the moment when Dan pulled up to make a delivery. Sometimes I would stay in the cabin while he went around the back to unlatch the van door. I would feel the slight rocking of the truck as he hoisted himself up among the sides of cows and the pigs hanging headless and hoof-less and hairless on their stainless-steel hooks. I would lean forward and peer into the side mirror. Then the truck would bounce again and Dan would appear in my view, bent over as he carried the carcass across the footpath and into the butcher's.

He always hoisted the carcasses onto his left shoulder, and I loved too the bizarre asymmetry of his white meat-coat, the right side always approximating white, the left side smeared with abstract patterns of red, like the smocks we wore to painting in the preschool group.

Sometimes towards the end of the day, when the truck was getting empty, Dan would ease up to the kerb, pull on the handbrake, turn to me and say, 'You can get out here, darl. We'll have a chat to Barry the Brick.' The old Erskineville butcher was a solid giant rectangle six-feet high by four-feet wide, and as red in complexion as a house brick. Dan would unclasp my seat belt and I'd lower myself from the phone books to the floor of the cabin, waiting for him to come around to the passenger side. He'd open the door and I'd dive, as if he were a swimming pool, into his arms. It was a game in which I always tried to catch him off-guard, and he always staggered backwards under my weight, saying, 'Whoa! Almost lost you!' He lowered me to the ground and I'd run to the back of the van. Dan would unlatch the doors and swing them open, press the button that lowered the hydraulic platform. Holding hands, we'd step onto the platform. Dan would look down, grinning at me. 'First floor: children's toys, ladies' haberdashery, grey socks, beach balls, perfume.' It was different nonsense every time, and I would giggle, just a little, because I knew the best was to come.

Dan would press the button. The platform shuddered and rose up to the level of the van. He remained poker-faced, in character. 'Second floor.' He would peer into the refrigerated darkness and do a double-take. 'Goodness gracious me. Second floor: dead pigs, dead cows, and buckets of blood.'

And I would holler and laugh and run into the gloom, slapping my open palm against the haunches of the pigs, whose skin was so stretched, pale and young, and who I never related to the happy animals of Marine Island. Standing in the semi-darkness among the swaying carcasses, I looked out through the open door to the bright hot shops and streets, the people walking on the footpaths like characters in a dream. It was delicious to bathe in the knowledge that I could see them but they couldn't see me.

When the last carcass had found its way into Barry the Brick's coolroom, Barry and Dan would often come out to lean against the truck and open a couple of cans of beer while Mrs Barry the Brick looked after the shop. I would sit on the patterned metal of the hydraulic platform, dangling my feet over the edge and swinging them lazily backwards and forwards. I felt that my presence on the platform spelt out to the passers-by a kind of proprietorship. The truck was mine—the business, too, of course—but more than that: the strangeness of it all was mine. I knew somehow that a meat van, so full of life so recently raw, was not the same as a bread van or milk van. It was in that league of *otherness*, along with, say, firetrucks or flower vans. The world of special things that glowed.

Occasionally, on a Friday, Uncle Dan and Barry the Brick would have more than one beer. The first can was always drunk quite quickly. But at the cracking open of the second can, I knew that I had a little time to go off exploring around the back alleys behind the shop. With the second can the day seemed to slow down, and I could sense the almost imperceptible relaxing of muscles in Uncle Dan and the Brick, the mild onset of serenity that came with the approach of the weekend and the first warmth from the first beers of Friday evening.

'Uncle Dan,' I'd say, 'can I go out the back?'

And Barry the Brick would reply, 'You go through there, love, and ask the missus to let you out through the packing room.'

I would glide into the shop, which smelt just like the truck but was less cold. Mrs Barry the Brick kept behind the counter a supply of lollipops, and would always try to delay me while she rummaged through the drawer looking for one. 'That's right, little one. Come inside from the sun. And are we having a nice day?'

'Yes.'

'We've been driving with Uncle Dan, have we?'

'Yes.'

'Wait a minute there, I've got something for you.'

'Thank you.'

'There. Do you want me to take the wrapper off for you?'

'No, I'll keep it. Thank you.'

I would clench the lollipop in my fist and imagine the slow release of sugar, later, in the truck, with the low sun flooding the cabin and illuminating every crack and fissure on the windscreen. We'd stand for a moment, the butcher's wife with her hands pressed together, myself staring at her apron.

'You're such a beautiful little thing, aren't you?'

'Can I go out there now?' I would ask, pointing out through the back door.

'Of course, of course,' Mrs Brick would say. 'Off you go, now.'

The backyard of the shop seemed to stretch forever. It was a place so full of junk that it offered unlimited opportunity for exploration. Above all, it was a place of exquisite privacy. The butcher shop was like a barrier, on the other side of which lay the world, which meant sunlight, and adults, like Uncle Dan. Uncle Dan meant the truck, and the truck meant the way home, and the world flowed on from there, Tom and Tess and everything that was familiar. But here in the backyard of Barry the Brick's, things had no purpose, and I imagined that everything just sat there, untouched, unvisited, day after day and all night too, for the long stretches of time between my visits. In the Bricks' backyard I came to feel, for the first time, that heart-fatiguing sadness that has nothing to do with events concerning the self but comes from the objects that surround us.

There were old car bodies to enter. There were stacks of wood and rusty lathes, a shed, a doorless refrigerator on its side. There were concrete pipes just wide enough to slither through.

I was the caretaker of this world. Everything was machinery. It was a world of complex forms.

Shopping with my mother in the supermarket once I'd seen a man in a long white coat, like Uncle Dan's but clean. He was moving slowly down the aisle and making ticks and numbers on a sheet of paper attached to a clipboard.

I'd watched him for a while, watched the way his total absorption seemed to isolate him from all other activity. It seemed to me that his job was important.

And that's what I did in the backyard: check things, tick things off. I did the rounds, talking to myself as I moved through the yard, imaginary clipboard in hand. Counting the beams of wood. 'One. Two. Three. Four. Five. Seven. Eleven. Twenty-six. Nineteen. Okay. That's nineteen.' Pressing all the buttons and knobs on the old car dashboard, in sequence, because it had to be that way. Crawling through the pipes and stopping halfway, resting on my back to inspect the cracks close above me. Imagining the whole yard alive with whirring and clicking, a functioning entity made workable and possible by me. An entity that craved my presence in all the weeks that I was away.

There was the cat, too, which I had seen several times but never actually touched. It kept its distance with a wary affection, always purring, as if wanting to come near, meowing incessantly but then moving away. I liked to think that the cat was in charge of things when I wasn't there.

One winter day when the yard seemed dark and sombre, I was checking all the meters and gauges. The sky hung heavy and added to the yard's greyness. On other days more summery than this the blueness of the sky offset the brittleness of the yard, and it only took a single bird, unseen, to sing, for my mouth to split for smiling. On this day I moved automatically through my tasks and was beginning to think of going back out into the street, where Uncle

Dan and Barry the Brick would be, in the normal world. I swung open the rusty door of the shed and moved into the darkness. I stood still, waiting for my eyes to adjust. I ran my fingers over the repeating contours of a stack of red terracotta roof tiles. Then I imagined spiders living in the crevices and pulled my hand away. The shed was boring. I went back outside.

In the far corner of the yard was a pile of old tyres that I had never fully investigated. It was an organic rather than an angular thing and so seemed out of place in the butcher's junkyard. I had thought of climbing the little hill of rubber once or twice but it was peppered with the gaps between tyres and the holes in the tyres themselves, spaces that led into the unknowable insides of the mound. I imagined dark and crawling things in there. It had always been easier to be Isabelle the Inspector, and to look after the factory than to go near this place of shifting spaces.

My eyes made one final sweep around the yard and a flash of movement caught my attention and brought my gaze to rest on the rotting wooden back gate at the furthest edge of the yard. The tufts of grass that grew around it showed that the gate had not been opened in many years. There was the cat, the uncatchable cat, a scruffy tortoise-shell, squeezing itself through a gap in the gate and landing silently in the rubble and weed.

It looked at me and meowed faintly, moved straight to the tyres and climbed to a jutting ledge that formed halfway up. I squatted and extended my arm, as if I held food. 'Puss, puss puss!'

The cat stopped and turned its head towards me. Then it turned away and slithered through a gap in the tyres and disappeared. A second later I heard a tiny chorus of squeals, like the faintest of sounds carried on the wind from miles away.

I knew at once that a new thing had unfolded in the yard, and I hoped now that Uncle Dan and Barry the Brick would drink many more beers, that their drinking and chatting would stretch on into the evening; that they'd forget about me for a while. A special event had arisen in my life. I moved gingerly to the hole where the cat had disappeared. I placed one leg on the lowest tyre and leaned forward, balancing my hands on the higher tyres and craning my head to peer in.

The cat, reclining, looked out at me and meowed again. Nestled into its wide soft belly were five or six kittens, the tiniest kittens I had ever seen. Perhaps I had never seen any until now; the moment lodges in my memory as a kind of epiphany. They moved continuously, pushing forward on their little twig legs, massaging around their mother's distended nipples in a rhythmic pulse. I reached my hand in and allowed the cat to smell my fingertips. I gently began to stroke its flanks, brushing my hand over the mound of kittens. I moved my hand beneath the belly of the kitten closest to its mother's head and detached it from the nipple it so furiously sucked. Its lungs emptied all of their air: a squeak no louder than the pips of a telephone could be heard.

I moved the kitten to its mother's purring mouth. The cat licked the flailing bundle of fluff; calmed, the kitten allowed itself to be buffeted by her tongue. Slowly I extracted my arm from the tyre cave. The mother cat made only a weak meow.

I held the blind black kitten to my nose. Bewildered by this new thing, the overwhelming breath of a four-year-old girl, its head moved in short sharp swings. I cupped it in my hands and rubbed it over my face, cooing and shushing as it continued its belligerent squeals. I cradled it in my lap, in the folds of my dress, and wanted the moment to last forever.

I ran back through the yard and met, at the back door, Uncle Dan coming through to collect me.

'Look, Uncle Dan!'

'What is it, Bumble Bee?'

'It's a kitten! Can I keep it?'

'Where'd you find it?'

'Over there, in that pile.'

We walked across and Dan peered in. 'Brand-new,' he said. 'Brand-spanking-new, they are. You used to be that big, you know?'

I crinkled my nose. 'I did not. That's stupid!'

'Hey,' he said gently, taking the kitten from me and placing it back on the purring mother's nipple, 'they can't be away for too long just yet.'

'Can I keep it, Uncle Dan?'

'We'll have to talk to your mother about that. Let's keep our fingers crossed. But even if she says yes, we can't take it straight away: it has to stay with its mother for a while longer first.'

After the longest few weeks of my life, Truly (as in 'Truly Scrumptious') came to be the Airly family cat. My cat. From his humble beginnings in Barry the Brick's old tyre pile, Truly became for the next thirteen years—he would die the same week Dad was arrested—the serene centre around which streamed the pandemonium of Airly life, the fortunes and misfortunes and the flow of time. And I became—at least for the next five years or so—Chief Cat Choreographer, dressing Truly in an endless array of bonnets and scarves and T-shirts, and moving his reluctant limbs to the latest Abba song, or to 'Don't Go Breaking My Heart' by Elton John and Kiki Dee, or 'Staying Alive' by the Bee Gees.

Dan

FOR THE YEARS LEADING UP TO THE WEDDING IN 1968 Tess and Tom and Dan remained all but inseparable. Tom finished his medical studies and for two years was an intern at Concord Hospital. Dan moved with an erratic kind of inevitability from one girlfriend to another, never getting too close, and in a marginally less erratic way from one job to another, never quite finding the one he thought suited him the best. ('That'd be a lifeguard on a deserted beach, wouldn't it, Dan?' Mum told me Dad said once.) Dan was a labourer, a warehouse storeman, a clerical assistant for one week—his first and last brush with the Public Service—and for a whole seven months in late '66 and early '67 a fibreglass sprayer in a factory at Ingleburn, far from the ocean in Sydney's south-western suburbs, which manufactured kayaks and canoes. I would always associate my uncle with the ways of the ocean, a connection based almost entirely (the mermaid tattoo was the other factor) on the blue kayak, scratched by moves from house to house, that rested on the kayak shelf Dan constructed in each of his garages.

For Tess, the physicality of Dan and the disconnected grace with which Tom stumbled through the world came together in some mysterious way to form a complete unit.

Tess adored Dan for his sweetness and his rough humour, his bull-at-a-gate determination, the loyalty and admiration he showed for his big brother. But she loved Tom deeply and romantically, and desired his body also. At the wedding, the very notion of the phrase 'from this day forward' was to Tess the promise of the great bounty of life rolling into the future and the thrill of not knowing what comes next.

Then I was born, as I have said, in 1969, and for some years Tess was occupied with my raising, with a domestic life whose boredom was offset by the intense pleasure of watching me grow and change. And Tom was building his career from lowly beginnings, working hard at his small general practice. Dan delivered bread for a few months in 1969 and the pleasure of driving a delivery truck stayed with him so that three years later, when he decided to get more serious about long-term employment, it was the meat-truck job that stood out in the Saturday paper.

Initially Dan took to bringing me with him on the shorter runs, a few hours in the afternoons now and then, to allow Tess some time off. On a Monday in 1973—I was four years old and it was more than ten years since Dan had first met Tess—he came over to collect me. This must have been around the time I found the kitten. I've pieced this together, a little of it from conversations with Tess, and what I don't know, I've imagined. Almost everything I tell here is fact. Very little is imagined. This next is imagined. Let's just assume that having played all morning in the back garden with the next-door neighbours' kids, I was taking my midday nap.

'Have you got time for a quick coffee?' asked Tess. 'It'd be good if she sleeps as long as possible.'

'A coffee, sure. I can spare a little while.'

When Tess dropped the teaspoon and bent over to pick it up and Dan's hand gripped her arm just above the elbow, the frailest faltering 'What?' emerged from her mouth. Then she felt a surge like electricity move through her body, and her ears burned uncomfortably hot as she stood fully upright. For no more than a second they stared direct and hard at one another. There was no thought, on Tess's part, of propriety, or loyalty. In the years that followed, the most surprising aspect of the whole thing for Tess was the absence of her consciousness of Tom for those first supremely physical moments.

They locked together, kissing. Tess loved sex with Tom, the languid abandon with which he grazed upon her neck, with which afternoon shadows fell, with which a new and delicious world opened out among the crumpled bed sheets. But she was not prepared for the urgency and the grasping for flesh that exploded there in the kitchen with Dan.

I'm imagining as I write this that she thought she might combust in the heat of it all, and that she experienced a moment of panic when she realised she hadn't breathed for fifteen or twenty seconds. She clasped his strong arms. Beneath her palms she felt the slight give of the huge veins of his wrists. He smelled sweet, of blood and sawdust. She ran her hands over his biceps and squeezed them. Suddenly she was aware of the moisture down south. What was going on? Her body was leading her now. She felt herself beginning to swoop, from a high cliff, wind-sheared, towards some unbearably pleasurable valley.

Wrong, all wrong. His electric hands on her thighs. They shuffled breathlessly backwards to the door, colliding with a corner of the fridge. They realigned the trajectory, down along the hallway to the bedroom. Tess stopped, pulled away. 'Wait. Wait.'

She looked into the child's room. My god, I'm talking about myself. She looked into my room. Lost to the world, I breathed softly, dreaming through goldness in the warm afternoon light, my eyes twitching. Tess turned back to Dan, pushing his chest to the bedroom door, fumbling with the buttons of his shirt.

And so began the affair. You want to know my opinion? Well, I wish it didn't happen. What can you possibly expect me to say, to feel about the thing? It seemed to be fuelled by a furious turbine: driven by a reservoir of compulsion. It was to become an unstoppable sequence of violent, sporadic couplings (four, five, perhaps six times a year) marked by guilt. It became like a drug: their resolve to stop was always at its highest immediately after each illicit, breathless meeting. Weeks or months later, when the opportunity arose, a desperate panic would subsume their limbs and loins, and nothing then existed but the need to have sex.

Tess knew she could somehow justify the fact of having an affair. It was the fact of it being... 'Fact'? I don't know why I bother to use the word. It was the fact of it being her brother-in-law that was the problem. She knew she had stumbled into a taboo world. She found three slim justifications. One day a few years back she mentioned these. It was the day she first told me, directly, about the affair, during a slightly drunken conversation in the kitchen. She told herself that life is short. This didn't mean that nothing mattered, only that when strange things happened there was often no turning back. She told herself that anyway it would end soon, and each time it happened she told herself this more firmly. She told herself that sleeping with both Tom and Dan Airly was really just like sleeping with two aspects of the same person, the softness and tenderness of her husband made whole by the compacted strength of his brother.

She told herself all this for six years and four months. Then she thought that the beginning of a new decade, the

1980s, and me soon to be a teenager, was as good a time as any to make changes, to begin again, to rediscover Tom, who by now was so lost in his work; who once had been her whole world, her love and her salvation and the vehicle of her flight away from Constance and towards the future. There came the day when Dan and Tess were alone, and when Tess said, 'Dan. Danny. No. That's it, forever', Dan knew she was speaking a concrete truth. He felt, like her, a strange relief, as when a storm has lifted and the bruised trees flutter their leaves.

It seemed it had been hardly worth it. Six years of pretending, punctuated by moments—only moments—of an intensity beyond normal consciousness. All the barbecues, the dinners, the Christmas holidays at Avoca Beach, the way Tom and Dan related, taking the micky out of each other, good mates as always, the way Tess went to bed each night, the way Tom read her moods and caressed her, the way I finished my homework and knew nothing. Yes, in case you have been wondering: I feel I knew nothing. The way in which Tess never stopped loving Tom, never felt repulsed by him, never stopped desiring him and making love to him all those years, never felt anything lacking in Tom that Dan somehow replaced, other than that hard brute fact of their drowning, of sex, which was only ever real in the moment it occurred, and therefore seemed hardly worth it. I might as easily have written 'seemed more worth it than anything', for later I was to find that drowning place. Sometimes it's hard to think of anywhere better.

Like I said: I feel I knew nothing. I knew nothing except what all children pick up who float unconsciously in the stream of time that is childhood, far below the surface currents of the adult world and illicit affairs: that love could be fractured and serve different purposes, and that intense love could be divided, between people just as easily as between moments of time. And this inner knowledge confused me, because it didn't match what I saw all around me on TV and billboards and in books.

Dan never stopped loving me in that beautiful world called Uncledom. After everything had ended with Tess, he finally married, nearing forty, and began to have children. He was aware, with a sense of unease bordering on guilt, that I was his favourite, even compared with his own children. He never told me this but there are some things so clear they don't need to be said. Nor did he ever stop loving Tess; indeed, it seemed to him that his love increased once the long affair ended, since it could continue from that point unimpeded by the burden of secrecy.

Nor did Uncle Dan ever stop loving Tom. Dan's trick was to compartmentalise his feelings and actions. Though what he had to build was less a compartment than a concrete wall seven feet thick. Kissing Tess, making love to Tess, his mind was overtaken—a kind of alien abduction, really—by the greater forces of urgency. Being alone with Tom—prodding the sausages at a barbecue, say, a can of Fosters in his hand—it must have been as if his mind had expressly forbidden the forging of any connections between sex with this man's wife and the man himself, dreamy and red-haired in the backyard sun as the barbecue trundled happily towards dusk. And as for being together with the two of them in the one place, which happened often enough, it was simple: Dan was like an actor in a trance. So those rare moments when he felt the frightening weight of his actions—I am betraying my brother's trust—clustered only around the immediate aftermath of the sexual act. Say, thirty or forty times in less than a decade. I suppose it's bearable.

And as for Tom, my gorgeous sad father, whose tragedy I am moving towards? There was something in his make-up that refused ever to confront a situation. I am piecing all this together backwards, retrospectively, hodge-podge. But I can state with absolute certainty, with the authority borne from being his daughter, that from the early days, with a sinking feeling in his stomach, he knew. Not the details, for he was operating on instinct, but the hard fact of the thing's occurring. It tortured him, how much he loved both Tess and Dan. He simply adored them. Yet no matter how hard he tried to raise the affair to the surface of his consciousness, he could not budge it an inch, and he could not in any way turn his love into anger, far less hatred.

Instead he plodded on through the years, working harder and harder. Fear of the poverty of his working-class childhood was reawakened, and the hidden distress he felt for six years transformed itself into the idea that if he could just earn enough money then Tess's love would return, fully, all of it to him alone. And this, perhaps, was the saddest part of it all. His search for money never repaired the love; rather it began the series of events that led to his final separation from us all.

The fraud began almost as an experiment. It was easy enough, in the beginning, a mere tick in the wrong box, to turn short consultations to long consultations on the Medicare claim form, and from there, very slowly, over months and years, to begin claiming for visits that didn't actually occur. There would have been a time when I could not have believed this had happened, when I could not write these words. But everything in this book happened. At any rate, the court records speak for themselves. I read them once, years after the event. Mum somehow retrieved them from the lawyers. It was like reading Primo Levi: I wanted so desperately to believe I was reading fiction. It is hard to account for the difference between what I saw in my father and what had really been going on in his life. I only loved one part of Tom; I thought it was all of him. In the court records another Tom arrives to frighten me.

He didn't particularly need the extra money; over the years he'd steadily built up the practice, and life had always been comfortable for us. Extra money meant better holidays, better cars, better dishwashers. Eventually it would mean a better house, which one day would become the house of whispers and of shadows, and in which, like an invisible rain of dust and darkness, my father's madness would descend.

But extra money would not bring back the past. You could not go back to 1973, to that moment on a sunny afternoon, and take Dan's hand away from my mother's arm.

It was all a pointless form of self-destruction. My mother loved our family, the linkages and the tenderness between herself and Tom, between the two of them and me. The affair with Dan was an entirely separate thing, and she tried to deal with that as best she could. On that day I mentioned, when she was a little drunk, she said, 'It was my problem. There was no reason for it and I don't know why it ever happened. It was nothing to do with your father. He never spent anything on himself. I guess all the material things were for you and me.'

'He gave us all this...*stuff*,' I said. 'But he lost his mind.'

'He was the man least likely to ever go to jail. The man least likely to ever do anyone wrong. Even the government.'

But all through the late seventies and into the eighties the momentum had continued to build for Tom, and each tick of the pen, each forged signature, each instance of fraud piled on the back of the other. When, in the mid-eighties, the Department of Health began their first great sweep of the Medicare system, Dr Tom Airly was, alphabetically, the first anomaly to appear on the graphs, the first radical flow against the general trends. He was a North Shore doctor—a silvertail, worse even than any Syrian doctor at Lakemba who systematically rorted the accounts—and the first of whom a thorough example was made. He was scrutinised for a year before the case was handed over from the internal fraud unit to the Federal police.

All the while Dan plodded along, driving the meat truck for nearly ten years until, at the age of thirty-six, the affair with Tess over, he too conceived of the idea that other changes might be possible. That's when he took the big plunge, made his first buying trips to Indonesia, rented a warehouse in Tempe, turned it into a showroom and filled it with beds and mattresses. That's how the bedding empire known as 'Airly to Bed' started, and that's how Uncle Dan became famous, through the cheap, late-night television ads he starred in, as the Futon King of Sydney.

Cross-bar

IN THE MEANTIME THERE WAS ME, AND MY OWN 1970s. While you tumble through the undercurrents of other people's lives, you start to grow yourself. Of all the girls in all my classes I always had the longest legs. On a baking spring day at the primary school sports carnival, nine years old, a collector of cicadas, a dreamer of eternal love with Luke Skywalker, I found myself falling upwards into my new obsession.

The high jump. Mrs Egan was merely rounding up numbers to fill out the event. 'You, Isabelle...and you, Cathy Cleary there, and Helen. Come on, girls, you're in the high jump.'

Everything else was fun on sports day—the break to routine under the sweltering sun, the cares of the world temporarily set aside in favour of a world hung with banners—so why not this?

Mrs Paul, the plump kindergarten teacher, was in charge of the high jump, a small cluster of activity in the centre of the field, well away from all the track events and the four camps of red, blue, green and gold T-shirts that lined the far side of the 100-metre track.

'All right, now,' she said, 'under-nines.'

I lined up with my red team-mates. I had never attempted this before and the whole thing seemed absurd. I preferred the expanse of the running track, that sense of wind and a bursting heart as I raced to break the ribbon.

When my turn came I followed the lead of the others, running in sideways to the high jump and jumping over the cross-bar with a scissor kick of the legs. It felt like nothing. But four jumps later, having won the under-nine girls' high jump and having beaten the boys' record as well, I was a little fonder of the whole event.

I lingered to watch the higher levels. During the under-eleven boys event I watched Toby Collins, who did Little Athletics, win the high jump Olympic-style, lifting his whole body backwards off the ground and sailing over, backwards and sideways. It was an extraordinarily graceful moment. I knew that I had found my sport. I fell in love with Toby, too. He was my first love—my first love, that is, who wasn't Luke Skywalker—though he was never to know it. In thirty seconds I had fantasised a complete life together: we travelled the world performing high jumps and being interviewed for television. We wore tracksuits on which were embroidered, in silver thread, 'Toby and Isabelle'.

Then the high jumps were finished, Mrs Paul had marked all the results on her clipboard and the under-elevens, Toby included, had dispersed.

'What are you still doing here, young Isabelle?' asked Mrs Paul, who had taught me three years earlier.

'Miss, please,' I said, 'can I just try something?' I pointed at the high jump. 'What was my best jump?'

Mrs Paul ran a finger down the clipboard. 'One metre, six. Why?'

'I want to try it higher. I want to try it different.'

'Isabelle, the event's over.'

'But Miss…'

'The event is over, love.'

For me, it had only just begun. I couldn't rest now. Something was expanding inside my head. The only way to stop it exploding was to get it out of the head and into the body.

'Miss, I think I can get a lot higher.'

'Hurry up, Isabelle. I've got to get these scores across to the tent. Here, quickly then. You take the other side. We'll try you at one metre, twelve. No, no, unscrew that— that's it. Now place the top at 1.12. Screw it tight again. The beam rests on that.'

The bar was set a full eight centimetres higher than my last jump when, grazed by my heel, it had wobbled for what seemed like a minute. But new methods invoked new hopes. I came in for the run-up, trying to remember the Toby Collins method of flight. When I leapt towards the jump I felt like the mountain goat in *Kimba the White Lion*.

I left the ground, felt all my muscles strain. The exhilaration of floating was a revelation, a new world opening out. I actually felt myself move towards the sky. It blazed blue across my vision, a wild blur of hemisphere. As I sensed my shoulder clear the cross-bar, I arched my body backwards. And your feet, lift your feet. I was finding my way in the world, through the air. Resplendent in my red T-shirt, awash in the ecstasy of that temporary weightlessness, I sailed through the H of the high jump. The horizon tilted and for a brief instant the brown streak of the administration building crossed my line of vision.

I landed in a roll on the soft blue pads and bounced my way back onto the ground. I threw my arms in the air and grinned at Mrs Paul. 'One more time! Higher!'

'One more. Then that's it.'

Each time up there, I felt a vast and giddy serenity. Anything was possible. The world could not contain itself. Four flights later, I knocked off the cross-bar at 1.18 metres. The unrequited love for Toby Collins—he was two years older than me, centuries at that age, and we never even spoke—would soon fade, but my anti-gravity talents were quickly noticed. The affair with high-jumping would last a long while yet, though ultimately it would be ocean and not air that would capture my heart.

They were supremely physical years: a blur of sports events, my body stretching and growing. A new kind of tide arrived when I was thirteen. Suddenly one day I felt wetness in my underpants. It was the last class of the day. The sun came in the windows at an angle through the gum trees that rustled outside in the slight breeze; Mrs Beck seemed dappled and indeterminate, far away at the front of the room.

At first the wetness only registered as a secondary thing. Seconds later there was nothing in that room but myself and my awareness of blood.

During the week I had felt queasy a couple of times, and twice had noticed a spot of red on my underpants. I came up with a bizarre theory to help me ignore what I knew to be coming; I theorised that somehow, on two separate occasions, something microscopic and sharp—possibly a fragment of glass that had found its way into the washing machine and then into my knickers—had cut me down there.

Put me in a school uniform again, put me back at that moment, and nothing, nothing at all is clear but the unmitigated fuzziness of everything. I felt I was swooping endlessly, at light speed, towards a blackness not even the light could reach. It wasn't terror, but a kind of wave, a moment of coming to. A realisation. *I am bleeding. I'm sitting in the science lab and I'm bleeding.*

How much blood was there? I had no idea, no previous experience to gauge by. I didn't want to touch myself. I didn't want to look. I shifted uncomfortably on the stool. I had to get out. I imagined that behind me the blood might be dripping over the edge of the stool. I stood up and moved purposefully towards the door, glancing back to confirm that the stool was dry and clean. I was already halfway across the room when I raised my hand and said, 'Miss! Miss! I have to go to the bathroom.'

In the locked cubicle I hitched up my dress. I stood with my legs slightly bowed, like a cowboy's, and I pulled the elastic of my underpants outwards and peered in at the thin, arrow-shaped stain of red. I sniffed the air, not sure if such a thing would have a scent. My panic rose again. How quickly was I bleeding? How fast was it spreading? I knew about tampons and pads, but no-one had talked about this, not my mother, not any of my friends except for Caroline, and we were like the blind leading the blind. Certainly not my mother. This was 1982. Perhaps it's different now.

Finally I touched myself. I brought my hand close to my face and stared at the mucousy smear of red, not as bright as I'd expected. I pulled out fistfuls of toilet paper from the roller, squashed it all together, crammed it into my underpants, pushed it against my wetness. I felt a little more secure now. I knew that even if blood flooded out, I'd be all right for a while.

I left the toilets, walked to the office and got some change for the phone. I had to ring my mother, even though the idea made me feel somehow ashamed. As I dialled the number I remembered Tess saying she had a busy day and would not be home. There was no answer.

Fortunately I had some money that she'd given me to buy a few groceries. The bell to end the school day would ring in five minutes. I didn't want to talk to any of my friends about this. Maybe Caroline, who was my best friend, but she was away from school today. I felt that the world was a huge metallic place.

My father couldn't help me. He was the magic man. I loved to sit in his arms, my head cradled against his chest, soothed by the rise and fall of his breathing as he watched TV in his favourite armchair. I placed my ear against his chest in the same way—with an expectation of mystery— that I would listen to a seashell. I imagined that oceans of wisdom were swirling inside him. But he couldn't help me here, doctor though he was. This was blood. This was something new.

I felt strange but strong as I strode from the school. It was a late spring day in Sydney and everything was in bloom, giving off a profusion of musky perfumes and a sense that the air was beginning to become heavy, as if preparing for the long sticky summer ahead. It was the kind of day in which I had always felt as light as air, jumping from the bus and running with Caroline through the back streets to our homes. At such moments even my school uniform seemed like an exquisite thing, a fabric made from wind and weightlessness.

But now it seemed that the world was heading in one direction (light) and me in another; a direction that was both lighter than air and heavy as blood. The future, I guess.

At this time of the afternoon the horseshoe of shops that formed Melton Street Mall was all but deserted. A few old ladies pulled vinyl shopping carts and one or two bored-looking young women pushed babies in prams. In the pharmacy I was relieved to see that the chemist on duty was a woman. A young girl, only a few years older than me and wearing a starched white uniform, crouched near the doorway unpacking a carton of eyedrops onto the shelves. The shop was empty of customers.

'Hello there,' said the pharmacist from behind her raised platform.

I hadn't thought about what I was actually going to say. I felt my jaw lock tight. 'Um, tampons and pads,' I murmured.

'Just here.' The woman pointed to a shelf.

I wanted to get out of the shop and home as quickly as possible, but I didn't know what to buy. And how far up should a tampon go? What if it wouldn't fit? What if I couldn't do it? In magazines I had read, there were more ads for tampons than for pads, so I figured that more women used tampons. I thought there must be a reason for this, that somehow this meant they were better.

I took a packet of each. Later, in the luxury of my own bathroom, I would work out what was best. I placed the packets on the counter. The pharmacist rang up the sale and gave me my change. I could feel where the toilet paper was a little wet against the inside of my thigh. I looked up at her.

'Are you all right, love?' she asked. 'Do you know what to do?'

I said, 'Yes,' and shook my head, 'No.'

'Mind the shop for a moment, Trudy,' she called to the assistant. 'Come with me.' She led me quickly through the back of the shop, past the storeroom and into a tiny bathroom.

'It's nothing,' she soothed. She stood facing me and placed her hands on my shoulders. She was a stout woman of about fifty, with wavy blonde hair and kind crinkles around her eyes. 'It's your first time. That's all right. The first time can be very frightening.'

She wanted to comfort me. I wanted her to go away. I wanted to be alone with the technical details. I picture myself standing forlornly in that bathroom; it was really just about blood, about inconvenience, and yet it was an event of pure spirit, in that the future, when thought of, is always abstract.

'I'll leave you to it, dear,' she said. 'I'd just use a pad if I were you. It's easier. There's a little pamphlet inside the packet that shows you what to do. It's very simple. You can decide about tampons later.'

Walking home, I tried to piece together all that I knew about menstruation. It wasn't much. I knew that once it began it would continue, regularly, for at least thirty years. I knew it was silly, but I pictured somehow a reservoir inside me, a thirty-odd-year allotment of menstrual blood. I wished I knew how much blood to expect: would it just keep flowing all day, or would it come in one deposit and dry up? I wanted to ring Caroline; I knew it hadn't arrived for her yet.

A sprinkler flickered lazily on the next-door neighbour's lawn, its rotating prongs sprouting a lovely looping pattern on the neat green. Something landed on my arm and I went to brush it away, but the flash of colour caught my eye: a red ladybird. I lifted my forearm closer to my face. The red of the beetle was a candy-coloured red, brighter and harder than my blood; it seemed to bounce the sunlight away from it. My blood was part of a more permanent and brooding world. So much had happened in an hour: this, too, was a presage of the future, that life could hold within itself such concentrated energy.

Around thirteen my mind kicked into gear also. I became an adult twice, in a sense. I discovered poetry; it's like some kind of virus that good teachers help you catch. There were never enough anthologies. It was wondrous, this world where words pierced the surface of things, a bigger world than I had known or imagined. The reading of poetry excited me more than listening to the music I loved. I didn't try to write it; I understood that it came from a realm that drove the mind further and better than anything else. Then I came across novels for grown-ups, as opposed to the class sets, so full of moral messages, that we used to be given; and my horizons expanded even further. In 1982 in the fiction section of the school library it began when I found *The Ballad of the Sad Cafe.* The copy had last been borrowed in 1971. Not only did I ache with the sadness of the book's events, but it almost broke my heart to think of the book itself, the object, the copy, its lonely vigil of years upon the shelves. And the great loss of all those students who never borrowed the book between 1971 and 1982. I would think, too, of the dust motes that floated through the locked silent library during the endless summer holidays. And every book yearning for its union with a reader. And it seems from then on I did nothing but read for many years. Read, and attend sports events. Eventually the reading took over. I remember the state championship selection rounds for the high jump when I was seventeen years old. I remember the sinking realisation that my heart was not in it. Competition no longer stimulated me. It was connection, depiction, perception, the recording of events that I wanted.

On my sixteenth birthday Dad bought me a Pentax. Another new world, photography: the trapping of light and memory and time, an endeavour so heavy with the sad grace of its own nostalgia, it can barely support its own weight. The notion that the earth too is weighed down with hundreds of thousands of tons of photos of itself and the things that happened on it—that holidays and people's

memories do not exist except insofar as they exist on film—
did nothing to hinder my furious energy as I joined the
photography club at school and became, at last, an Artist.
My Year Eleven major work was called 'Ecosystems of the
Sidewalk Cracks'—a series of studies, taken with a zoom
lens, of the weeds that grew in the footpaths of my suburb.
I printed the photos in black and white then hand-coloured
and framed them, drawing complex arrows and inform-
ational text on each print, which was accompanied by
detailed, mock-botanical reports of the landscapes, including potted histories of the miniature aliens who inhabited
them. More than a decade later, with that same Pentax, I
would record the texture of the stonework and masonry of
the buildings of Paris, fine details of cornices and lintels
and statues (but never the full statues)—everything just
graphs of light, life at its most abstract, as I wandered full
of anxiety and the absence of Matthew Smith. It is funny
how details can help us so much, and how things begun
in jest can come back and make more sense than ever.

It helps to focus. Later my father would focus on science, as his mind began to go. Perhaps it bought him extra
time. I took on all my endeavours obsessively, driven from
an early age by the sense that every minute, every detail,
counted. Too much of this may not be so good. When you
let things go, the relief is immense. For Dad the immen-
sity was death, so it's hard to say how much he knew, in
life, about relaxing. There is said to be a state in which
tension disperses through the shoulder-blades, through the

cortex, and evaporates in the benign air. It's long been my intention to live there.

For a long time, anyway, the high jump was like the road home. I loved to win, of course—there was a pure thrill in that. But it was not the main event. The thing for me was the weightless moment high up in the sky when the mind was blank and empty—empty of all detail, you see—and the whoosh of the wind was all that there was.

And how, I came to wonder, as I went through a particularly moody period of angst during those teenage years (I was listening to The Cure a lot; they were big at the time), was it possible to feel love with an empty mind? For if the mind was empty, then it was empty of love too. In the high jump there was no world but the world of air that I—my body—moved through. High above the cross-bar in that moment of time smaller than a blink, my awareness of my own self disappeared. Making room for everything: everything felt, heard, learnt, known. Love was all that existed then, a joyful sense of vertigo and my love for Tess and Tom.

Love and Loyalty

AND IT WAS EXTRAORDINARY, THE FEELING OF LOVE IN our little family. (Extraordinary, too, that possibly I had it all wrong.) I knew nothing but safety and warmth. That seems all the more extraordinary now when I consider my mother's growing up. She was born into the great gulf left by John Carter's disappearance. The wonder to me is not that she made it through at all but that she made it through so relatively intact, so vibrant. So free of bitterness and so empty of resentment. Though later she would know all about regret.

There is wonder to me also in how my mother could view Constance with such tenderness and compassion. Perhaps it was only tolerance. I know that Tess's teenage years were a sterile time of endless 'tasks,' afternoons of sewing and cooking and cleaning, a time of dark foreboding, when everything was done in claustrophobic proximity to Constance. Tess was even banned from joining the youth group of the local church. It was a potentially dangerous place; boys could be there under false pretences. The Cold War was outside, was everywhere. The world seemed to be held together by not much more than anticipation of looming catastrophes.

And like the ugly duckling, my mother did nothing but remain still, and patient, for a long, long time. This level of patience is inconceivable to me; I could barely ever wait for tomorrow. But the sixties emerged and the light began to rain down upon the century. The beautiful John F. Kennedy had a face that glowed out at you from the newspapers. My mother had waited out the years, and then, without rancour for Constance, she glided towards the future, and love, and loyalty, and Tom Airly, my unbearably handsome father.

And everything started so beautifully. And later it all went so wrong. Why am I not surprised at this? It's hardly as if I'm writing a mystery here. And yet it's all a mystery. If I could find someone to blame, perhaps I could get angry. Anything would be better than this sadness, this sense of regret for events that were never mine.

Of course, there's no prerequisite for a Constance to make things off-balance. Much of what I remember is made up of breezes on which there float the scents of jasmine,

and golden evenings with Tom and Tess. It is not all darkness. But Constance: that was a darkness.

There were no gaps in those vast monologues that con-
stituted her entire world. They were solid blocks, dense
with matter, like buildings. I was no more there to her
than any of the rest of us. I was a sounding board against
which to hear better the echoes of her own voice. From
an early age I began to resist going to her house. There
was a darkness around her, unpenetrated even by the television's glow. I would sit and listen, captive as a babysat
child; later, I was reluctantly captive again, as an adolescent
on compulsory visits.

'The cyclone! Well, how could you possibly be prepared?
When the war was over, it was hard to believe that anything
bad could ever come again. That long, long war, and all the
men away. John Carter—let me tell you, he was handsome—came to visit me in the dress shop in 1942, in April.

'"I'm off to fight the Japs," he said, "but when I come
back, I'd like to marry you."

'Just like that. Three years later I was nineteen, going
on twenty. The Yanks dropped the bomb on Tokyo and
then the bad half of the century was over and the good
half began. The bad half and the good half. Do you get
what I mean? But I was wrong! I had it exactly the wrong
way round. John Carter came back. We were married in
January of 1946, four years after he proposed. Well, he had
me then, and off he went again. How was I to know how
things worked?

'I saw him for four months of that year—a month in Sydney, three on that horrible island, without even a proper house—and I came back to Sydney for Tess to be born, and the cyclone came. I wasn't even there at the time. Thank God. But it swept into my heart and uprooted everything. And then what's left? The stillness. And Tess with no father.

'He didn't die, you see. No palm tree crushed him, no sheet of corrugated-iron roofing decapitated him. He chose the cyclone to flee. I mean, it was the event that set him free. All those letters, all those excuses—*not long now, my darling...it will all be ready soon...soon, dear Constance... the boys are working hard on the bungalow*—and then the cyclone and then one letter and then I never hear from him or see him again. Someone from the copra company told me they thought he'd mentioned America. After a couple of years I stopped looking. Why bother? He didn't want us.

'And now I know that all men are like this: unknowable. It's just that in some cases they stay longer. And what then? They stay. All right. That's good. They stay. They're in the house. That's their body there, moving through the rooms. And the daughter grows up with an unknowable father. What difference does it make? Better the way it was for Tess, I suppose.'

Given the opportunity I would have begged to differ. My admiration for Tess lay in the way she had navigated her way through the sterility of childhood. Blame: we could go back forever. And yet I can't help but see, in the origins of what Tess did, the dark stain of Constance's psyche. As if, denied so much for so long, Tess would without even knowing it want everything. And Tom and Dan, as I've already said, were the two halves of everything.

I am, perhaps, paying too much attention to all the details of this affair with Dan. I just don't know. It's true that much of what I remember is a kind of harmony. I think of long stretches of my childhood, of growing up, and I remember the three of us, my parents and me, an inviolable unit of warmth. Maybe it was beginning to change a while later, maybe when I was ten or twelve and off in my own world. Everything happens after a delayed reaction. From 1973, when the affair began, to about 1978, my dad was home a lot. Evenings were a wonderful time of homework consultation and games and television and, in spring and summer, long hours playing in the backyard. As the affair neared its conclusion around the end of the decade, we began to see less of Dad. We had it all and then we got some more: more cars, a new house, this one with a swimming pool, a luxury apartment on the Gold Coast each Christmas holiday. And I didn't care about any of it. Or at least I took it for granted. It was other things that made me happy: high-jumping, poetry, photography. And just being with my mother and father.

My father's delayed reaction was this hunger for money. I grew up in the undercurrents of a stream that was already flowing towards its doom, twenty years before the dam burst in Dad's head on Mount Kilauea. I was happy enough in that stream. I did well at school. There was sport. The company of friends. I am told I was a girl who laughed a lot. I roll tape and my memory confirms this. The print of my past is immaculately crisp.

And later, I piece everything together, and it's horrendous. What happened? My mother, Tess, and my uncle Dan set in motion a series of events that led to my father just...resigning his commission on the planet.

The affair had ended when I was about eleven. My father spent the late eighties and 1990 and '91 in prison for Medicare fraud. Around '92, I began to live with Matthew Smith. One day in late 1996, when I was twenty-seven, only a few months before Matt died, my mother told me all about it. I remember feeling dizzy for days afterwards.

We'd spent the afternoon shopping; it had become, over the years, a pleasant way of spending time together. Later we always chatted and gossipped while we unpacked the groceries. When Dad went to jail Mum had gone back to nursing. She was a senior nurse in the emergency ward of the local hospital and loved her job with an enthusiasm even other nurses found intense. Often I had to ask her to tone down her graphic descriptions of the day's events. Her empathy for the suffering of others was boundless. Other than work, she seemed to do nothing else but paint and draw. Her sketchbooks were bursting with the most vivid colours, perhaps the very ones that were being bleached slowly from Dad's world.

We'd finished unpacking. I was drinking iced tea. Mum made herself a gin and tonic. She wasn't a big drinker. One was enough to put a red flush in her cheeks; halfway through the second one she was a little more tipsy than usual. I have forgotten many things in my life but I will never forget the way the cold droplets sweated off our glasses that afternoon and pooled on the kitchen table as shafts of sunlight moved through the room. I will never forget the blue-tongue lizard I had noticed out the window as it sunned itself in the garden. Nor the incredible weight with which my mother's soft words entered my ears.

I don't even remember how it began. Perhaps I had mentioned Uncle Dan's upcoming birthday; let us assume it was that. Dad was so lost by now. This was only three years before the end for him. Perhaps, because Tom was so lost, the mention of Dan was enough to spark something off in my mother. Maybe she had wanted nothing other than to offload the secret.

'I suppose you guessed way back then about Uncle Dan and me?'

My heart suspended activities for a few beats. 'Guessed? Guessed what?'

'Oh dear. Worse than I thought.'

'Mum? You're kidding me, aren't you?'

'Oh dear. Maybe we can just rewind this conversation.'

'Mum, what are you saying?'

She took a deep breath. 'I thought you might have known,' she said. 'I just assumed…'

'You and Uncle Dan?'

'We had an affair. A tiny affair.'

'Wait. Wait. A tiny affair *when*?'

'When you were tiny. When you were a baby. A couple of years old.'

'For how long?'

'Not long. I mean not much. Too long. But hardly ever. A few years, I suppose.'

'A few years. And Dad knew?'

She sighed again. 'I guess he does. Did. He didn't want to know. He didn't want a confrontation about it. Maybe that's why he and Dan don't make so much effort to see each other these days. Maybe it's a delayed reaction thing.'

I poured her a third gin. I wanted to hear more. I don't know if at this moment half-remembered emotions from my childhood were beginning to make sense: confusions, uncertainties, the registering of tensions.

'But how did it *start*, Mum? How exactly did it happen? The first time?'

'Issie, I don't know. All I know is that five seconds before it started, I didn't think it was about to happen. I had never thought of it. It had never entered my mind. And it wasn't like disloyalty to your father.'

I felt a surge of anger. 'That's bullshit, Mum. What is it if it's not disloyalty?'

She stared at me, stunned. Her eyes filled with tears. 'Oh, Issie—'

'No, it's just—'

'You're right. You're right. But in the beginning I loved the excitement of it. I don't know. It was crazy. I don't know why it kept going.'

'And Dad never talked about it?'

'Not really, no. I tried once. He didn't want to talk. He said, "It's in the past, it's over, it's nothing." And when it was happening, if he'd ever brought it up, I would have denied it.'

'How often did you…like, how often did you *see* Dan?'

'A few times a year, maybe. For a few years. Completely insane. And I loved it. But I regret it. And I can't help thinking it's the cause of everything that Tom's become today.'

'Oh Mum, don't be silly. Dad's not well—that must have been bound to happen anyway.' I didn't believe a word of it. I just didn't want her to cry any more.

It was all information. I didn't want to ask about the *feelings* of the thing, about abstractions. That was too much to know in one afternoon. That could take years to sort out. From the rest of the conversation I might have got clearer dates, that's all. Those are the dates I've tried to piece together in this story. Oh, and she told me about the three reasons, which I've mentioned earlier. The three reasons for continuing with the affair. Something like: life is short; sometimes you can't turn back; surely the thing will end soon anyway. Kind of like one reason, in a sense. The awful thing is, I think I can understand. I think I can imagine how that might happen, how a direction, a momentum, could begin from a seed and grow into something nobody could have predicted. I think I can see how Tom just sent everything deep inside. It's like a cancer, the kind a doctor could never find. But he was his own doctor, and in the end he could only remove it himself, up there in the heat of the caldera with the baked lava canyons all around him. A specialised operation. For every gain there is a sacrifice, and the removal of the parasite sometimes entails removal of the host. Well, that is just as well; and it is clear at any rate that he took himself far away from us.

What if this, what if that? If there were never any Dan? It is also clear that only in the here and now, on the path of events, are we measured against circumstances, and that hypotheses are flimsy in the face of what actually happens. Tom is dead now. Every word I write takes him further into the past. Yet I remain assailed with an unrequited longing for his presence.

Arrest

B UT I HAVE GOT AHEAD OF MYSELF. WHAT I REMEMBER now is that I couldn't bear to see the fear and sorrow in my father's eyes, the day the police came for him. What I remember is one of these moments when everything goes cold, when the heart overloads and the whole world changes.

My final exams were looming and I felt a strange buzz of anticipation about university next year, a wide new world away from the incestuous claustrophobia of high school. I was trying to work hard. I was seventeen. Looking back, I see that all the bursting impatience of adolescence had some- how transformed itself into that infinite patience, a kind of grace, that is liable to descend on students in the home stretch of high school. To an outsider, it might have looked as if I was in some Hindi trance of ecstatic calm. This was not the case. The grace was a survival mechanism that helped me focus until the exams were over. I wanted good marks, the best possible. Uncle Dan had said to me, when I was thirteen, 'Study hard, Issie. Education is knowledge, remember that. And knowledge, as they say, is power. We all need some of that.'

The notion had stuck with me. At thirteen I thought that power meant strength and I knew I had that—I could jump higher than almost anybody—and I never wanted to lose it. At seventeen I was beginning to see also that power was not just something that resided within, a potential energy called strength. It was also the power to choose. At this point I still couldn't decide between studying literature at university or painting and photography. Either way, the choice seemed a pleasure.

And so, despite the palpable tension I'd felt in the house for some time (not a result, I realise now, of the Dan under-currents still flowing deep beneath everything else six or more years after the affair had ended, but rather the loom-ing criminal investigation), despite the unexpressed fears between my parents, I sailed through eight months of intense concentration and rigid study that were somehow bearable.

And then, with only two months remaining until the first of the exams, the night arrived when the police knocked at the door.

I was upstairs studying English. *This sense of evocation and observation presents many readers with the difficulty of deciding whether the 'I' of many of the poems is voicing the personal attitudes of the poet.* I was reading well beyond the night's homework, preparing for an essay. *The moonlight transforms the scene, making it appear a harmonious whole and, as it dissolves some of the features of the daylight world, so it dissolves the usual ordered process of memory and the poet surrenders to a different, more random principle of association...*

I heard the knock at the door; I wasn't expecting anyone and it didn't mean anything. But after a few moments I was shaken from the poetry by an unfamiliar keening sound moving up the stairs and past my bedroom door.

I opened the door. My mother moved past me on the landing, hands to her face, her fingers trembling uncontrollably, a soft wailing coming from some place deep in her throat.

'Mum! What is it? What's going on?'

She didn't look at me, as if eye contact would cause her to crumble. I followed her into the bedroom. She was opening cupboards and pulling out drawers.

'Mum! What's going on?'

'They're arresting your father,' she snapped, and fell to her knees at the chest of drawers. 'I've got to get him some pyjamas! And a toothbrush. You get the toothbrush. And the toothpaste.'

She was quivering. I couldn't take it in. 'Arresting? Mum, what do you mean?' Then my feet were moving before my brain had done a thing. I raced out the door and down the stairs. 'Dad! Dad!'

My father was sitting perfectly still in the leather armchair, each arm lying symmetrically on the armrests, like a sphinx. On the couch were perched the two detectives. All three stood up as I reached the bottom of the stairs. I glanced at Tom; he seemed to be looking back at me with something that resembled sorrow. I looked at the two other men. They were blank-faced, awkward.

I stood there, suspended in time.

'This is my daughter, Isabelle,' said my father.

The older one, at whom I was glaring, nodded politely.

I turned to Tom. 'What's going on, Dad?'

'It, er, appears that I'm being arrested, darling.'

The older one reluctantly spoke. 'Your father is under arrest for conspiracy to defraud the Commonwealth Government in matters relating to the processing of Medicare claims.'

My vacant mind was trying desperately to create some detail. I stared at the patterns on the carpet.

'Isabelle...' my father said in a strange quavering voice. I looked up into his eyes. 'It's all a misunderstanding. It'll be cleared up in no time. It's a dreadful misunderstanding.'

'But where are you going? To jail?'

'We're just doing our job, Miss,' said the detective. 'Your father will be taken to the North Sydney lock-up tonight. He has the right to a lawyer of his own choosing, or to Legal Aid. Bail can be applied for tomorrow. Whether it's granted or not isn't up to us.'

'But he didn't *do* it,' I pleaded.

The older detective shrugged.

'You'll have to talk to your father about that, love,' said the younger one.

I looked again at my dad. My own wide eyes could have devoured his. It was all about eyes, the truth.

'I'll be back later tonight or tomorrow,' he said. 'You look after your mother. It's all a storm in a teacup. A colossal cock-up.'

Tess came down the stairs, still trembling, clutching a pair of pyjamas I'd never seen before. They were blue, with a gold fleur-de-lys motif. The young cop tried to hide his smile.

'That's ridiculous, Tess,' said Tom. 'I'll be back in a couple of hours. Just give me the toothbrush.'

We both moved forward to hug him then. He kissed Mum once on her wet cheek and me once on each eye. I was too much in shock to be crying.

He pushed us away and composed himself, pulling the white cuffs of his shirt from his coat sleeves. Tess collapsed on the couch and I stood there, face to face with Tom.

'I'm sorry,' he said, his voice almost a whisper.

But I was looking into his eyes and could see that he was really saying, 'Help me.' Everything changed. Everything would be different from this point on. I would be on my own. They say that's what the final exams represent: the passing into adulthood. Well here it was, a month or two early. A premature birth, I guess. I cannot even begin to imagine what he was thinking at this moment.

Trying to keep a hold on the concept of relentless failure. An exhausting undertaking. I loved him, and had never had reason not to. And here I stood, in my self-obsession somehow taking his crime as a personal affront. I just can't imagine what was in his tortured mind.

And they took him away. It was very civilised. No handcuffs.

We were solid people, sound, as they say: trustworthy. My father had made some mistakes with paperwork. It was hardly like robbing a bank. I must be remembering the comments my mother made that night. We talked until 4 a.m., by which time my father's hastily located lawyer had secured bail. But I went to bed before he arrived home. It was becoming apparent to me, as I talked to my mother, that my father had in all likelihood committed a crime. The knot I woke up with in my stomach was crippling. I looked around at the walls of my bedroom and was struck by the sickening feeling that they were collapsible. Exposed to cyclonic winds, my bed would be torn from the room, me trapped in it.

The exams passed in a blur. There was a coldness in my approach—it felt like coldness was spreading through my veins—that resulted in lucid answers for English and History, in a clear logic that made Maths and Physics a breeze, French and Biology problem-free. Without seeming to concentrate, I ranked in the top 10 per cent of the state for all subjects and found myself free to choose from a range of university courses.

In the meantime, lawyers and solicitors were hard at work and the trial was continually set forward while preparations were made for a defence. I tried hard to take no notice of all this. My father's name was in the papers. I shut myself off from my fellow students. I drifted through life in the Airly household as if it were not my own. I drifted through exams, through my father's endless phone calls, through his stunned silences in the armchair, in a kind of reverie. I began to pay greater attention to loud live music, experimentation with drugs, and boys. In this life away from all that was happening at home, I felt most acutely my physical body; previously the exquisite pleasure of inhabiting a body had come to me on the athletics field, in the high jump. Now, away from home, I began to see that a happiness unconnected to my parents might be possible. It was a notion that until very recently had been far outside of my consciousness.

I'm not saying I knew nothing of my sexuality before any of this. I'd been discovering myself from the age of thirteen. There had been the boyfriends, the 'Will you go out with me?'s, and all that graceless fumbling. Gradually it got better, but it was clearly nothing more than practice. I lost my virginity, under only moderately disappointing circumstances, at sixteen; and already by seventeen I was getting an inkling of how good things might get. I'd dreamt through all my childhood of what I might do with my life. There was high-jumper ('Toby and Isabelle'), architect, archaeologist, then photographer. But now I began to await with excitement not what I would do but the someone that I, Isabelle, might possibly be.

The house we lived in became the House of Whispers. It surprised me, the ease with which I made the transition from believing in my father's innocence to understanding the fact of his guilt. It surprised me to suddenly see court cases as tactical battles rather than arenas of absolution, of the restitution of reputation.

After fourteen months the case was heard and my father was sentenced to six years' imprisonment, with a non-parole period of four years. For a few days the papers editorialised: was he the sacrificial lamb or was it a case of greed getting its comeuppance? Opinion was divided.

I was reaching the end of my first year of photography and print-making at art college, had moved out of home and into my first shared house. Prepared though I was for the outcome, I cried on the day of the court case. But the next night, dancing in a nightclub, the idea came to me— it may have been the strobe light that did it, or possibly the Ecstasy—that I could begin the process of trying to forget, and move into a new world. I wanted to make my own way. Clearly my father was not the whole universe. He was merely my father. It struck me that forgetting everything would be a pleasant thing, as this new world descended more gracefully upon me than other people's sadnesses and the heavy sadness of prison cells. Then a friend introduced me to Stephen, lean and angular with a mop of dark hair, like Shaggy in *Scooby Doo*. We had a drink, we danced for a while, we went home to his place, and spent the next ten months together. It wasn't that I was replacing one man with another, though retrospectively it looks like that. It's just a coincidence that as my world was beginning to expand, my father's was contracting.

And yet it was as if my life was split in two. It is so tragically easy to see that now. Tom wasn't retrievable then nor ever again. I think that I coped with what happened by trying to hate him for a few years. I tried to show this hate by visiting him in prison as rarely as possible; on those occasions I did visit, with my mother, my folded arms and sulky silences would invariably collapse, at the visit's end, when I would fall into his arms and cry into his chest. I longed to be nine years old again, but knew that being nineteen and twenty and twenty-one was its own kind of power, and that horizons unfurled, though not forever.

The other side of my life was…well, it was bounteous, benign. I practised doing what adults did, and wondered if this was love, my time with Stephen. Good practice, at least, in the matter of lust. On musky summer nights in my twentieth year, when legions of fruit-bats were screeching and flapping through the skies over Sydney and the soft breeze blew ripples through the mosquito netting, I would feel deeply the elegant satisfaction of being caressed by that gawky boy, and I would take his face in both my hands and kiss him hard, as if I could draw from those lips the very strength and sweetness he did not know he had.

The Ticking of the Clock

WHEN TOM WAS RELEASED FROM PRISON AFTER FOUR years I was twenty-two years old and many things had changed; indeed, most days I felt nothing but the future, a violent wind slamming into my face. And every event that tumbled towards me seemed a pleasure, if for no other reason than its newness. The past was beginning to seem like a town across a river whose bridge had been destroyed, but there was a dreadful sense of anticlimax and a painful choking of emotions at my father's return.

In the first months after his imprisonment the thought had been that all of us would hold our breath and Tom would be out before long and then everything would return to what it had been before. But life had long since flowed on.

The first Sunday lunch after his release was a good sign that there wouldn't be too many more. It certainly didn't feel like they were about to become a weekly or even a monthly event. Grandmother Constance was there, surprisingly pleasant for a change in her attempts to make vacuous conversation. Dan and his family came. Dan drank too much, as usual. When we were all seated he said to Tom, 'Jeez, it's good to see you here, like this, mate. I bet freedom feels good, eh?'

Most of the conversation focused on my studies. I struggled hard to add colour to my art college life, to an environment I really only visited for the purpose of delivering essays, using the darkroom and hanging out with my friends. My real life took place at night, in the crowded inner-city pubs where my favourite bands played. I felt that college was all but over, and that I was an unknown, unformed thing. I could barely express this to myself, let alone to Tom.

There were silences during the lunch. The foreboding of things to come. Tom seemed to be having trouble concentrating. I noticed his new habit of staring hard at salt shakers, wine bottles, walls. A small furrow, like an arrow pointing downwards to the bridge of his nose, had appeared between his eyebrows. I'd never seen it during the prison visits; maybe it was the lighting.

Tess brought a jug of water from the kitchen and stood behind him, stroking his hair. She wrapped her arms around his neck and leaned in close to squeeze him. 'It's so wonderful to have you back.' He smiled and his green eyes flashed. In them was the handsome carefree father swinging me around the backyard. I became giddy with the vertigo of the sudden shift to five-year-old-ness. My face flushed.

Between the main course and dessert there was a lull. Dan lit a cigarette and leant back in his chair. Constance rabbited on about the unseen creatures attacking her garden in the dead of night, and how the different snail and insect repellents contained acids that corroded the skin on her hands and possibly also thinned out her hair. This was only a couple of years before she died, God rest her tortured soul. Tess went to the kitchen to whip the cream. Tom placed both hands on the table, as if to steady himself. He began to stand. 'I'm very sorry. I just have to lie down.'

Acting according to some unspoken etiquette, Dan and I stumbled to our feet.

'Oh—listen…you do whatever you have to, big Tom.'

'Are you okay, Dad?'

'Yeah, yeah,' said my father, offhand. 'I guess I'm just not fully myself yet. Tess, love!'

Mum poked her head around from the kitchen.

'I'm going to lie down. The meal was beautiful. I'll give dessert a miss.'

'Are you all right?'

'I'm fine, I'm fine. I just really haven't adjusted yet. New rhythms, new habits, I guess.'

He turned and started up the stairs, and at that very instant I understood that he was already a ghost, that the molecules that made up his body were beginning to disperse at the edges and blend with the atmosphere.

Over the next few years I came to visit the house less and less. Curtains were drawn more often so that even on the brightest blue of Sydney summer days the inside of the house was like a cold, still mausoleum where the dust had settled forever. It was the house of a considerable part of my childhood and yet it was not at all the way I wanted to remember my childhood.

Often Tom was sitting in an armchair in the dark and staring at the floor. Any attempt by Tess to open the curtains was met with wrath. All this was anger I had never seen before. It was as if the man, my father, had changed so much that only his appearance was the same. I can't say now if accepting this change was in some way more difficult than coming to terms with his death. This was the first death.

Why do the angry become so verbose? From the kitchen one day I heard Tess start to pull open the curtains, and my father's harsh, 'No!'

'But you need some sun, Tommy.'

'There is, I believe, my dear, a veritable fucking universe of sunlight outside these four walls. The garden, for instance: from memory, it's absolutely awash with photons. Luminosity so thick you'd choke on it. If I wish to expose myself to such freewheeling airiness, I'll go outside. In the meantime, I like this room the way it is. Do you think you can grant me this one indulgence?'

With me he avoided such confrontation. One time I swung the curtain open, catching him unawares, and said, 'What you need, Papa Bear, is Vitamin E.'

He smiled weakly and said, 'You're probably right. You're probably right.' He sat blinking and unshaven in the arm-chair. 'My beautiful Bella—you probably know a lot more than me now.' I pictured all his brain cells shutting down and felt the flush of goose bumps on my arms.

Five minutes later he had left the room to go upstairs and take a nap. He never slept in the main bedroom any-more. He had moved a camp bed into his study and nes-tled there among his pillars of books.

I made tea and sat down at the kitchen table with my mother. The kitchen abutted the sunroom and had become the designated area of light on the ground floor.

'It's beyond a joke,' said Tess. 'I don't know what to do. It's a psychological condition, you know? It's called depres-sion.' I reached out and stroked her hand.

There was only ever one time I tried to talk with him about what had happened, about the Medicare stuff, about why. It was a conversation that faltered and barely got started before it finished. It was a relief to change the sub-ject. And with my relief came the feeling that I wouldn't try to go down that path again in a hurry.

I had said, 'You wanna see a movie, Dad?'

'Not today, love. I'm not really in the mood.'

'But Dad, you've got all this freedom now, you can do all these things you couldn't do in prison. Let's get started!'

'I know, you're right. I just don't seem to have the energy right now.'

'But you've got to start doing things for the energy to come back. You can't wait for it to arrive.'

His resistance was incredible. I sat on the edge of the armchair and hugged him hard, but he patted my back as if paralysed by awkwardness. In the middle of attempting to hug him, a memory entered me.

I was four years old. It was the year before school began, and we were picnicking in a park. There was a tiny pond.

'Mum,' I said, 'can we throw some money in and make a wish?'

'It's not a wishing well, dear, it's just a pond.'

It was perhaps three metres in diameter, less than a metre deep. I moved away from the picnic blanket and over to the pond.

'You be careful, Bella,' my dad called.

A concrete barrier defined the circumference of the pond. I stepped up and spread my arms to gain balance. Tentatively at first I began to sway my way around the circle. I picked up speed, leaning inwards as I ran, feeling the thrill of the water rushing beneath me on one side and the blurry earth on the other, feeling power and pride at my own sense of balance.

Then my sandal slipped out from under me and the thing I thought I could defy was happening.

Parts of the memory, as I sat for long seconds in that stiff embrace, were vague—I couldn't remember the water coming towards me—but what was vivid and immediate was the immersion. I was flailing in the panic of drowning and loss.

I had been unable to sit myself up out of the water. The surface of the pond had been a thin still film but now I had disturbed it. I'd been on one side and now I was on the other. From the underside it occurred to me that my mother and father would know what to do and where were they, could they please come? I could make out the clouds in the bright sky, and over to my left the tree I'd been climbing twenty minutes earlier, but everything was shifted and stretched and distorted, a terrifying parody of the world of clean edges I had known to that moment.

Still I couldn't raise myself, though my arms were flapping so wildly I might have flown out of that water, a hundred metres straight up into the air, trailing streams of pond behind me like long arcs of transparent seaweed evaporating on contact with daylight.

At last there loomed a shadow above me, my father all fluid, the shape of his head to the left of his shoulders, his arms seeming to pulsate at odd angles from the dark central mass that was his torso. Although it was an alien shape, I recognised him from the shock of red hair. What was a moving towards unconsciousness felt like sleep, the beginning of a dream. Everything was all right.

The shadow of my flame-haired father expanded until the colour that resembled the sky was blocked. Then a force that came from nowhere clamped onto my tiny arms. It was the only thing that felt strong in that underwater world of weakness where I could not move. I was pulled upwards and the film of water broke up and peeled off my face. The world took shape in all the ways I knew. I coughed, and drank in the sky, huge gulps of it.

My beautiful father was hugging me, his chest a great expanse of kindness. My mother was stroking my hair. 'There, there. Bella, little Bella, it was nothing.'

I was blubbering but together they made me laugh. I was back!

'Look at you,' my father said, rubbing my cheek and pushing my face into his warm neck. 'You're a bedraggled little duckling!'

I looked down at the forlorn strands of my hair and my dress. It was a kind of liberation, to be in such a state and yet not be in trouble. I continued to cry but I began to giggle as well. In my wetness was a memory of life closing off, and I thought how I could lie clasped in the abundantly strong arms of my father forever and ever. My beautiful father, the red-haired man. If I stayed there I could breathe. His arms were like sofas as big as clouds. It seemed I thought these things not through my head but through my exhausted limbs.

And now? The man had walked away into another dimension. I stood up.

'Dad...why did you do it? The Medicare?'

'The what?'

'The Medicare.'

'Why do you want to know about that?'

'I don't know. I just do.'

He sighed, pinched the bridge of his nose. 'It just happened, you know. Stupidity. Greed. Idiocy. It just kept happening. You get lazy, you don't think.'

'But in the beginning? What happened then?'

It was not a loaded question. This was a few years before Tess told me about the affair. It was about getting closer: knowing more about him, finding him again.

'Gee, let me see. It's an awfully long time ago, Isabelle. Feels like someone else's memories.'

'But tell me anyway.'

'Darling, it's too far away.'

He leant forward, slapping his hands together with patently fake enthusiasm. 'It's too far away and it's too bloody morbid, little girl. Now grab the paper, the movie page. We're going to see a film.'

That was the one film we ever saw together in all those years, between the time he got out of prison and 1999, when he died. *Dances With Wolves*. Well, at least it was three hours long. Almost like seeing two movies, really. I cried at the end and Dad held my hand while the credits rolled. Really I was crying for him.

And on raged the storms inside his brain as the years unfurled.

Almost two years to the day after his release from prison, he was re-registered as a doctor. Through the long bureaucratic battle it was Tess who did all the paperwork, all the petitioning, all the legal manoeuvring, presenting pages for Tom to sign. On the day the letter arrived confirming his re-registration, he hugged her tight and sobbed once. He rented a consulting room and quietly opened up shop as a general practitioner, far away in Parramatta. He must have begun keeping the diary around this time. We found it in his papers after he died, along with the mad notebook of the suicide week, to which I am coming.

What amazes me is that for a few years he tried to describe what was going on in his head, when for the rest of us it was a lock-out situation. He drove across town to work each day and sat for hours, flicking through magazines, awaiting patients who never came. People have their own doctors; people stick to their habits. It was some years since his name was prominent in the newspapers. I guess people have long memories.

But a trickle of patients began to arrive, almost all immigrants, from Vietnam, Hong Kong, India, Indonesia. The Davi family from Bombay became his most regular customers. I suppose they must have mistaken my father's catatonic listlessness for serenity. His diary tells me he was grateful for their visits, for the company, the friendship and the sharing they represented, and on days or weeks when they didn't come he would drive home through the peak-hour traffic with a gnawing hole in his stomach.

And now he began to overservice and undercharge, the opposite of crime. Was he making attempts to redress for the other life a lifetime earlier? He didn't actually invent illnesses for the Davi children, but given the smallest excuse he was careful to monitor their progress, sometimes two or three times a week. He refused to charge for all but the most essential visits. He came to love the robust warmth of the family: gentle Mr Davi, trained as an engineer in India and now working as a stock supervisor in a Microsoft warehouse; his wife, so exotic to Tom in her ruby saris and bangles; the four children, two boys and two girls from two to nine, their Australian accents, the boys' obsession with rugby league.

Tom treated each visit, every patient, with meticulous care. All the while he was freezing himself silent in the dark depths of home, he was with concentrated tenderness attending to his motley new band of patients so recently arrived in the sunny glare of the bigoted old country. He loved them all the more for their knowing nothing of his past. His diary became a bizarre mixture of doctor's notes, introspection and the contemplation of his patients.

THUR 15th

10.15 Mrs Tang—compl. shortness of breath on
exertion. Trial run Ventolin puffer (samples).
Return 5 days.
10.30 Henry Kazik—travelling Laos, Cambodia—prescr.
doxycycline.
11.05 Euphonia da Costa. Daughter (Ines, 3)—pers.
cough. Sugg. syrup and return if worse.
These idle hours. Boredom might be a kind of crime.
Think of the starving children?!! Reminder to bring
good book. Boredom leads to thoughts of double-

glazing—consciousness of traffic. Consciousness *as* traffic. Lead poisoning a lose–lose sit'n.

11.25 Raoul Wu—11 sutures removed left elbow. Re-dressed Melonin & bandage.

11.40 Uri and Ida C.—prescr. nicotine patches x 2! Both ready for another try...

Raoul Wu—strange name. Borrowed? Anglicised? Accident happened kitchen of restaurant where he works. Why back of elbow? I picture illegal gambling dens, tempers raised.

12.00 Lunch. Perhaps I could be more like Don Quixote, believe this is all glorious stuff, the highest calling, utmost importance. Cheese and tomato sandwich: banquet of the gods. Raoul Wu: mounted on golden steed. Henry Kazik: Marco Polo. Mrs Tang: my fair damsel, my Queen.

Crossword.

1.40 Me: Knight of the Long Afternoon...

Cryptic crossword.

2.05 Pino Alzado. Soccer training—ankle. Swelling. Pain. Bound—crepe bandage. Refer Westmead Hosp—X-ray; prescr. Panadeine Forte.

If time stood still, and we could choose the time, the best time, then love without pain would be all I know. Tess on the beach, Tess changing the station on the car radio. Swinging Isabelle around and around in the backyard. Isabelle grinning at the Easter Show, the fairy floss bigger than her head.

Dizzy with love and regret.

She's an adult now. She's a busy girl.

2.30 Mrs Dekker cancels. No more appointments today. Call Tess.

It is hard to be positive.

He was slipping away, but slowly. Only the Parramatta patients were happy. The rest of us, I guess, were making do. For my father, the hours of work were squeezed in tight by the endless time outside of them. Each morning from Monday to Friday his mind rearranged itself to face the task at hand, and each evening he disarranged it. At the point when the Davi family moved away to Adelaide after two and a half years in Sydney, Tom felt that the hollowness, gathered together in a raggedy bundle and placed on a scale, was heavier at last than all the substance that made up his life. His image, not mine.

He reduced his working week to Tuesday, Wednesday and Thursday. No point in fighting the numbers any more. 'It's only for a while,' he told Tess. 'I can't stand the traffic snarls. I'll just take it easy.'

In the diary I find something that astounds me. At fifty-one years old, alone in his room on a Thursday afternoon after surgery has closed, he injects himself with morphine for the first and, so far as I can make out, only time. It must have been that vistas of unparalleled beauty opened up behind his eyes. This page, the morphine page, stands out because it is an entry in which his writing suggests a kind of peace. His body is warm, he says, and the world is warm, and everything fits together, as once before it did. But when might that have been? he ponders. For four hours he nods at his desk, immobile and filled with the light of tranquillity. I imagine the phone ringing and Tom Airly waking slowly from his deep nod. It's Tess, worried.

My father composes himself. 'Sorry, pet. I fell asleep. Paperwork.'

But somewhere in the distant background, behind this golden man whose blood was filled with eternity for a few hours, somewhere even in the middle of the morphine, was the man who knew that the peace was a peace that had not been earned. On the next Tuesday, after the interminable length of his long weekend, I picture him taking out the vial of morphine and weighing up the odds. Morphine, he surmises, will repair his mind at the cost of his life. A beautiful swap: perfect, noble. Restitution to completeness. He must have been thinking of Tess and me. He must have taken stock: he would have an oceanful of the desire to keep using the morphine, an egg-cup full of the desire to stop, a thimbleful of the belief that he could. He would certainly have had access, until medical records and accountability caught up: therein, no doubt, would lie the race between a second deregistration and death.

And here is a supreme moment. Surely it must have been like this. He puts the morphine back—there it is, just like that. It is back in the safe. He resigns himself to the loss of his mind instead.

The diary entries ended soon after this. The episodes began to roll into his life, like lumbering breakers in the winter storms at Ulladulla beach. Help me, Isabelle, help me, Tess, he cried out at night, deep in the middle of his troubled dreams.

Love Calls You by Your Name

WE ARE ALL, I REALISE, EVEN AS I WRITE THIS, MERELY moving closer to our deaths. At the end of this sentence I am closer to mine than I was at the beginning. It's relentless. It's a savage thing. And yet for a long time I've carried with me a sense of life opening out. Evidently it's some kind of protective illusion.

Certainly this sense was rarely more vivid than in those first years of buoyancy after I had obtained my gloriously useless Fine Arts degree. It is easy to look backward and see my father moving inexorably towards his darkening horizon. But when I think of myself at twenty-two, I remember only that feeling of growing lighter and younger, and how it seemed that the opaque weight of the world was dissolving.

Caroline, my friend through so many years at school, had long disappeared from my life. It had been as if suddenly, after the Year Twelve formal, a switch was flicked and the walls of school dissolved and those who had been intimate friends through the bizarre eternity of childhood were teleported into an unreachable dimension. When school finished I went straight to art college, as I've said, and she backpacked around the world, working and travelling for a year and a half. We saw each other a little when she came back but already the gulf seemed vast. She knew what she wanted to do and I didn't have a clue. She got a job with a merchant bank and moved to Melbourne, enrolled part-time in Business Studies courtesy of the firm. She told me her aim in life was to one day have at least nineteen million dollars, nineteen being her lucky number. God knows she is halfway there by now.

I had grown into new circles of friends, from art college, and from the bands that emerged out of it as harder evidence of the college's existence than any oil hung in an exhibition, and from the pubs where we gathered to drink and watch these bands play. It was during this time that I met Louise, the flamboyant centre of a circle of young women whose carefree solidarity I secretly yearned to be a part of at the same time as I kept my distance. I admired her greatly and perhaps also was a little jealous, with that haughty suspicion that the solitary have of the social. But one day we wound up talking at the college cafeteria, and we simply fell into each other's lives without any other preliminaries. It seemed we had been friends forever. She had black hair and dark eyes that sparkled. She welcomed me into the dynamism of her warmth. Over the years we became inseparable, shared everything, all trials and tribulations, all dreams and fears.

And so a year after university had finished, when we'd been doing nothing much more than working in bars and staying up all night and playing musical chairs with the boys in our scene, we took off, just the two of us, on a whim, right across the continent, by bus, to the empty west coast. I can't even remember what sparked the idea, or who thought of it first, or what we expected to find there. I'd heard about the dolphins at Monkey Mia: maybe that was it. There was both a sense of the exotic and of the absurd in operation—that there could even be a place with a name like that, in the middle of nowhere on the edge of the Indian Ocean somewhere between Perth and Broome; and that it could be a tiny town famous for only one thing: the dolphins that gathered each day in the shallow water by the jetty, among whom the tourists could stand, patting and feeding them. I was a little bit more of a cosmic cowgirl then than I am now, with a twenty-two-year-old's wish for all mysteries to be true, so it wasn't too hard to imagine some kind of 'special connection' making itself apparent over there, thigh-deep in the lukewarm water with my oceanic soul-brothers and sisters.

We got our first taste of western hospitality when a Perth taxi driver agreed to drive us the ten hours north to Monkey Mia for $250; he wouldn't mind fishing for a couple of days, he said, and then he'd drive himself home. Monkey Mia was nice—it was beautiful, standing in the water as the dolphins nudged your legs, running your hands along their streamlined musculature—but it was slightly less, I thought, than a mystical experience, waiting in line with all the other tourists beside the baking carpark crammed with campervans.

A family we met in the Monkey Mia caravan park gave us a lift the few hours back down to Geraldton, a fishing town of some twenty thousand inhabitants. By now we'd heard about the Abrolhos Islands, the coral islands a few hours by boat from the mainland: austere, serene, deserted, with only small settlements of fishermen's huts. It was in search of some derangement of the senses, in landscape so unlike the east coast, that we decided upon the Abrolhos as our next destination.

We met some of the local young fishermen. It wasn't hard; they flocked to us. They all had names like Skeeter and Pablo and Mad Dog and Hoots. Louise and I took the cue, delved back into the S. E. Hinton novels we'd both loved as teenagers, *The Outsiders* and *That Was Then, This Is Now,* and began to introduce ourselves as Ponygirl and M&M.

It was a big money year for the cray industry. The boys would throw wild parties, thick with a mist of sweet ganja smoke, overflowing with bottles of whisky and vodka and kegs of beer. Then at four in the morning they would stagger off to make it somehow to their boats, to begin the day's work. In the early afternoon they would return home, sleep for a few hours, then party all over again.

I was sleeping with a guy called Blitzer, Louise with Skeeter. Or maybe it was the other way around. He had a lovely body. He told me guiltily he had a girlfriend in Perth. I said I wasn't jealous.

It was a mad couple of weeks. I'd never been a big pot smoker, but in Geraldton, at a time when my life was suspended between possible directions, it seemed to make sense, and after a morning joint the day was fluid and comic and the immense hard sky became less menacing. I got an afternoon shift in the pub. My Blitzer boy's guilt got worse, not better. I ended his misery by suggesting, 'Let's just be friends.' Louise rang home to find that her application for a job in a graphic design studio had been successful. She would have to drop out of the Abrolhos plan. I decided to stay on for a while.

The first time I went on a cray boat, Blitzer's skipper picked me up at 4 a.m. on the night of a full moon. I stood on the deck as we headed out to sea from the Geraldton docks, marvelling at the way I only needed to tighten my calves to keep my balance up and down through the soft roll of the waves. I breathed deeply in the salt breeze. The fat yellow moon was setting out over the ocean, and then the sun began to rise back east above the mainland. For about ten minutes the two discs were aligned, each just above its respective horizon. I felt for a moment that I was truly in an inverted world where all experiences would be new.

Then the moon was gone and the sun grew smaller as it climbed and the morning began to take on colour. The water all around us turned from dark grey to silver to a luminescent green. I was delighted to see the flying fish erupt from the water, amazed at the distance they covered in air as they whirred like wind-up toys. I watched over the railing as a dolphin tracked us for a minute or two, cutting through the water with immense power. It seemed I had left behind a complex world—Sydney and art college and all the scatterings of my past and fragments of my present—and come here to a land of propulsion.

And then I met Terry Breen—it was nice to come across someone who *didn't* have a nickname—and his wife, Emily, and their three beautiful children, Charlie, Jack, and Laura; and through Terry I would come to meet Matthew Smith— ah, we've arrived there at last, almost—who for a time would become the love of my life. Love of my life. Love. Of. My. Life. A retrospectively absurd concept since the most I can say is that he was the love of a particular *period* of my life, and that it is the random vagaries of life itself, and never love, that define time limits. Meaning, to be in love and wish for its immortality is energy unwisely spent. The idea that we have any choice in the matter is the great illusion.

I met Emily and Terry at a party one night. I was attracted to their quiet presence. We got on well. They invited me to stay in the spare room in their house. I was sick of my caravan already and it sounded like a great idea. Terry was always gone hours before sunrise. On the mornings when Emily worked in the library I took the kids to school. On her days off we drank tea and she told me all the wild west sea stories and I helped her paint the renovations. She was thirty-six, tiny and blonde with a bright wide smile on her pixie face. She seemed no older than me. It was a shock to conceive of her as a mother. She might have been the kids' older sister.

The house was rambling and cool. Emily had orchestrated the renovations so that walls and ceilings had been knocked out and a high cathedral ceiling exposed. On days when the stifling dry easterlies blew, the house was always an oasis of pleasant breezes.

In the few weeks I stayed with them I came to love this family, its gentle warmth, the absolute devotion of each member for the other. Terry was reserved at first, softly spoken, but as I came to know him he came out of himself, and there flowed from him quietly and smoothly an endless procession of sea tales. I was hypnotised. The kids, who had heard them all before, still sat around him rapt, as interested in their father's retelling as they were in the reactions of a new visitor. We played Monopoly and watched bad television as the long evenings darkened. The local ads were all for four-wheel drives.

Somewhere between the first couple of weeks of parties and the next couple with the Breen family, I slowed down a little. In the space and the stillness I took stock of my desires. In the presence of their love I sensed my loneliness, and I understood for a moment, clearly, that deep and basic human desire for companionship at depth. I was twenty-two and had been with perhaps nine or ten boys in the past five years. I suppose I was thinking it was time for something *more*.

I had enjoyed my day on the boat with Blitzer and his skipper. So when Terry Breen asked if I would like to come out, I jumped at the chance. In the pre-dawn light at the dock where the *Storm Cove* was moored, as Terry and I climbed down onto the boat, Matthew Smith appeared from the darkness of the wheelhouse unravelling a coil of rope. I could make out nothing but the barest outline of his hulking form.

'Matt the deckhand,' said Terry, 'Isabelle the babysitter. She's here to keep an eye on things.'

'Hey,' he said softly, reaching out his hand and shaking mine. The first thing I ever liked about him was the sweet sound of his voice.

As the light came up I stood out of the way, watching the skipper and his decky at work and enjoying the soft undulations of our journey out to the first cluster of cray pots. Terry steered the boat, keeping an eye on the global positioning satellite navigation screen, where the location of each pot was marked with an 'x.' Matt prepared the bait on the deck, cramming the cowhide and the rancid-smelling herring and scalies and kangaroo meat into small plastic bait-traps inside the heavy wooden cray pots. I watched him, fascinated. Barefoot, legs spread for balance, head bowed in concentration, he worked methodically, cutting off chunks of the compacted cow skin, mixing it in with the oily fish heads.

I thought I saw whiskers, possibly eyelashes. 'That's not...' I said. 'That's not...shit, that's not a cow's face, is it?'

He glanced at me. 'Usually it's just the skins. Every now and then we get a box full of faces. It's the way they come from the abattoir.'

'Yech! It reminds me of something bad. *The Silence of the Lambs.*'

He unfolded one of the faces fully, held it up with his hand inside it like a glove puppet. The cow's face hung from the end of his arm wearing that same ridiculous look of incomprehension that they carry with them in life.

'The silence of the bulls,' he said, straight-faced.

'Aww, put it away!' I laughed.

'Gross, isn't it?' he said, scrunching it onto the bench and slicing off its snout. Then he looked up at me and smiled. His heavy plastic apron was smeared with the stains of fishguts.

It is just that moment that is hard to think of, to write of. In the photo album of memory there are snapshots that pierce the heart and from whose sudden jolt I am left bewildered and exhausted in my despair. In that smile I saw his warmth and shyness and loyalty, the whole courteous depth and range of his goodwill and calm grace. Or maybe that is just what I see now, in the uselessness of memory, which reaches only ever to where we cannot be. It is all such a fog. Trapped inside the windowless walls of the present, I cannot reclaim that moment on the deck.

He was tall and lean from his time on the boats. Later, in Sydney, when he fleshed out a little, he would remind me of a giant teddy bear. He was square-jawed like an actor. His unruly black hair was always falling in the way of his eyes. From a distance you would expect him, somehow, to have black eyes, but in fact they were crystal blue, with that extraordinary transparency you see in the brittle winter skies over the Blue Mountains, and in them, indeed, it seemed that tiny birds might be soaring forever on the rising corkscrew currents of air. There was a dimple on his chin. All this description is only love. Well, that is the way that he was, that I saw him. Not a word in this book is untrue. Everything happened just as it happened.

He didn't speak again for hours. I watched them work all day in the blistering heat. Terry leaned over the railing and hooked with a steel grapple the orange-and-white foam floats that marked his pots, then wound the rope onto the automatic winch. The huge pots lumbered up out of the water, sometimes empty and dripping, sometimes filled with the rustling and clicking of the lobsters all crowded together. I was enlisted for the day to move the cursor on the global positioning screen, erasing the 'x' where the pot had been pulled and inserting a new one at the next drop point. Matt tipped out the crays into the cakka box—cakka was the name for undersized crays—and measured them quickly one at a time. The cakkas would go back into the sea; the others were tossed into the steel-mesh tanks that rested in salt water beneath trapdoors on the deck. Now Terry would steer for the next 'x' while Matt picked up another baited pot, staggered under its weight to the railing and waited for Terry, checking the echo-sounder for likely good spots, to give the shout 'Go!', at which point Matt dropped the pot over the side.

At the end of the day we drew up at the dock of the fishermen's co-op. A forklift delivered the next day's boxes of bait and cowhide at the same time as a conveyor belt, lowered over the deck, took up the day's catch in orange plastic trays. Terry signed the clipboard passed down to him by the forklift driver. Then we moored further in at the *Storm Cove*'s berth and walked along the network of gangways until we reached the carpark. The ground seemed to sway. I went with Terry in the ute. Matt waved and we parted with little more than a 'Nice to meet you!' But I knew we would be seeing each other again.

He came to dinner a couple of times at his boss's place. Maybe Terry and Emily were setting us up. I got to know him better. He was twenty-seven and had been working on the cray boats—or during the off-season on trawlers down south—for nearly two years. He was from Sydney—this news pleased me—and was out here on a mission: to save enough money to go back soon and start his own small band management company. He wanted to be able to pay a year's rent up-front and to set up an office. I would come to learn that he was methodical like that. In later years there were times I would wish he was more impulsive. At any rate all our habits and traits and quirks come to nothing, in the end.

In his early twenties he'd played guitar in a band that released a couple of singles that made it halfway up the local independent charts. I knew of the band, kind of thrash-pop-fuzz like the Ramones with a surf theme, and had even owned and liked one of the singles, though I'd never seen them play live. Matt left the band, he claimed, when he realised that the combined mass of the members' egos had come to grossly outweigh their actual talents and success. Besides, he said, he knew he was never going to be any great shakes at the guitar. For a couple of years he worked at running the small Sydney office of a Melbourne record label, Buzzcut. Ground up, he learnt a lot about the business. He was all but managing the label's Sydney bands when he decided that he'd be better off doing this for himself, and doing it properly. He'd heard about the good money to be made on the Western Australian trawlers and cray boats and had come over, knowing no-one, to try his luck.

He hadn't mixed much in the pub life of Geraldton. Over there, in the cowboy towns, alcohol could effortlessly soak up all savings. He'd spent a quiet eighteen months, he said, doing not much else than working, sleeping and reading books. He was certainly, I noticed from the start, an obsessive reader in the widest range of subjects I'd ever seen, including my own great love: poetry. Now he was pretty much cashed up; his goal had been achieved. He was going to do the three-month season on the Abrolhos Islands, a few odds and ends back in Geraldton, then call it a day and head back to Sydney. He had been keeping in touch with events back home and had a couple of young bands in mind, including one who had sent a demo to Buzzcut but had never been signed.

There was his younger brother Peter, too, and his band Spud Gun. Peter was nineteen now, had continued to send Matt demo tapes, and it was clear that Spud Gun had emerged from the inchoate mess they had been as a high school band.

'You know,' Matt said one day, in his understated fashion, 'I think they can be big. I think I can help them get there. I know the ropes. I like the idea of looking after my little brother, too. He's smart, that's no problem. It's just that he's young.'

In these early weeks Matt never made a move on me, nor I on him. From my point of view I knew it would come, so I felt I could relax. From Matt I learnt later, with great amusement, that he thought I was unattainable and hadn't even bothered torturing himself with the possibility. It is so exquisitely funny and sad, the way we view each other; how very little, despite our best efforts, we communicate. But I was flattered to have been elevated to goddess status.

We barely knew each other. Everything smelled of the possibility of love. Terry asked if I would like to come out to Big Rat Island for the three-month season and be the cook. Four of the boats would pool their money for my wages. I would be cooking for ten men—Matt included—and have my own fibro hut.

'I think I'd love to,' I said.

It is easy, off the Western Australian coast, to begin to fall in love with the ocean. Everybody *likes* the ocean. But to love it is to feel that boom forever in the chest. In the journey out to the Abrolhos it is easy to drown in a blueness that on land is otherwise impenetrable, impregnable and always 'up above'. In the formless expanse of ocean and sky it is easy to feel comfortable with the swooping sense of vertigo that results from the sudden realisation that either there is a god and if so he or she infuses this place too, or there is no such thing and the atmosphere is indeed a frail membrane inside which, in the blue light scattered everywhere by air molecules, we can nonetheless feel moderately happy to be here at all.

It is all ocean. I sat on the prow of the boat, my legs dangling over the edge, as it cut through the rolling swell. The islands are so flat, with a maximum elevation of about three metres, that it seems you must have hours yet to cover, and then suddenly you are upon them. The first thing you notice is a change in the swell: the waves roll quicker and choppier as the boat nears the reef. Then I was looking at a row of huts that appeared to stand up out of the surf. On the sheltered side of the island were the rickety jetties. We moored and when Terry cut the engines there was not silence but from outside the reef the roar of the surf which would become, after some days, the same thing.

I wouldn't have gone if I hadn't liked Matt. He was obviously still blissfully ignorant of this fact. But I was immensely interested in exploring the possibility of falling in love with him. I sensed it would be exciting to find out if we could get along. On the very first night, made slightly braver by the joint I had smoked after dinner, I took a deep breath and walked from my hut and down the crunching coral path to Matt's, the last one of the row. He was in bed, reading by the light of a kerosene lamp, and seemed a little surprised to see me.

'Hey Isabelle,' he said softly, rising up on one elbow. 'What's up?'

'Oh, nothing much,' I said, almost losing my resolve. 'It's just... I don't really like my hut.'

'Ah... Oh, okay,' he said, fully sitting up now. 'Right. So... that's all right. Would you like to swap? We can swap huts. I don't mind. They're all the same to me.' I couldn't work out if he was genuinely thick, or just blind in his awkwardness.

'I don't really want to swap, Matt. I just thought it'd be nicer if I stayed here.'

I watched his thoughts pass across his face like slow-moving clouds. And then, as a late arrival, the bright sun of his enthusiasm.

'Sure! Great! No worries...er, well, I'm going to stay in bed here because I haven't got any clothes on.'

'Well, I'll just take mine off, then. And that'll make us even.'

For three months I felt as light as air. We didn't talk much. All the boats worked hard, long hours, seven days a week. I was left to wander the tiny island all day. I swam in coves where the water was so clear I could see every pebble, every fish, and the contours of the coral formations. I drew in my sketch book images whose simplicity could in no way capture the stark minimalism of the bare landscape: bleached coral and a bleached sky, a few tussocky dunes whose curves added an almost hallucinatory focus of detail, and the emerald encirclement of ocean in all directions. Out here it seemed that the top of your skull came completely off and the wind roared through, leaving very little room for thought to gain a foothold.

In a depression between the dunes I found the only place on the island where the endless clamour of the surf almost faded away, and my mind would spin at the sudden drop in sound. Sometimes in the late afternoon, when the sun was low enough that the hollow was in shadow, I would lie down there on the sand, look up at the sky framed perfectly by the ellipse of dune and think about nothing at all.

I went through all the books in all the huts on the island and wished I'd brought more with me. I'd always expected James Michener to be bad but I was surprised at just how unreadable he actually was.

The grocery runs came back well-stocked with whatever I ordered. The kitchen hut was abundant with supply. My imagination ran wild with the daily preparation of dinner. I invented dishes I never knew existed and we lived in a greasy-fingered feast.

For the first time in any relationship I felt no rush. The work of a deckhand was so utterly physical, and the hours so long, that often Matt would be deeply asleep within minutes of flopping into bed. At other times he would seem alive with electricity and we'd make love long into the night. Always, afterwards, as I drifted into sleep, he would lie on his side and trace his fingers all over my body, the lightest of grazes, in gentle repetitive motions, a kind of hypnosis of the skin. It occurred to me that my body was empty like a black and white page in a colouring book, and that his fingers were brushstrokes, or the flaking of crayons, and that were he to continue his tracing each night then eventually I would become complete.

We learnt little of each other during these three months. I barely wanted to. There would be plenty of time to talk later. On the island every event seemed suspended in a separate reality from that of the mainland. I found myself sometimes wanting to be back on the mainland, in case the urban Matt was different, so that I would feel safe enough to open up my voice and to let go of that flood of stories we tell each other when we embark on a journey. Later I discovered that he'd been dying to talk during those twelve weeks on the island, but that without any prompt from me he had decided that the best and most polite course of action was to return silence with silence.

I think it may have been in Kalbarri, before we ever got back to Sydney, where the next phase began, where love commenced to enter. It was in Kalbarri, his long two years almost over, that we began to talk, and all the words entwined themselves more passionately than lips and arms. In Kalbarri I saw him for the first time away from the sheer exhaustion of work. It was like a door opened up to the inside of him. I felt myself relax and grow even calmer with the concept of his being in my life.

We were back in Geraldton. The Abrolhos season was over. I was ready to return to Sydney and Matt planned only a week or two more of helping Terry do some end-of-season maintenance on the boat.

'I don't know what's going to happen in Sydney,' he said. 'I want it to keep going. I mean, I'd like it to keep going. That's my, ah, hope. My desire.'

I nodded, smiling. I found him so attractive in his awkwardness.

'But first,' he continued, 'let me show you Kalbarri. Terry'll give me three days off. He said he wouldn't mind a short break himself, spend some time with his kids. I'll drive you up there. It's very different from Geraldton. It's pretty beautiful.'

'Let's go now,' I said. 'I'm ready.'

Kalbarri, a tiny fishing and holiday port sixty-six kilometres off the main highway that runs on through to Monkey Mia and beyond, was an hour and a half drive north from Geraldton. Terry Breen had fished out of

Kalbarri for most of his life; it was only in recent years, as his children grew older, that he was forced to move to Geraldton, where there was a high school. He gave us the keys to his house. He was unconditionally generous, as was Emily, as the children would no doubt become.

It had been a spell of dry weather in the west but we turned off the highway and drove towards Kalbarri under gathering clouds. The two-lane road was lined on either side with a bright-red shoulder of dust. In all directions grew low hardy scrub. I had seen photos of the moors in England and was reminded of them now in the eerie darkness beneath the thunderclouds beginning to bunch. The day was still hot.

'Weird weather,' mused Matt. 'I don't know how much it rains at this time of year. Sure looks like it's going to.'

Scattered across the landscape were native flowers in bloom, bizarre and enormous like giant, bright-pink cauliflowers. We saw a kangaroo nibbling at a shrub by the side of the road. We slowed down to watch and it loped away unhurriedly as we passed. An old Beach Boys tape played on the car stereo. A while later we saw another kangaroo, dead several days and bloated with gas, its neck broken by the impact with a car, its mouth twisted open in a grimace. At exactly the moment we came over the hill and could see in the distance the ocean, the first splats of rain began to hit the windshield.

I have no idea where personal mythologies come from and I'm sure my own is not unique, but I took it as a sign that the whole sky relaxed and the scorching day was flushed away by the cold air and the storm. It was good to be alive, to be with Matthew Smith.

Again, the whole Breen sensibility flowed through the house in Kalbarri, five times more lived-in than the house in Geraldton, and therefore five times more lovely. The yard was a wonderland, filled with tyre swings and an intricate three-level treehouse. Terry had even constructed a flying fox from a high tree to a lower one. Inside the house the high ceiling fans hummed and the air washed past the back of my neck and the noise of the rain drumming on the tin roof was like a massage for the brain. We made love straight away.

Later we drove back out through the national park, back the way we had come into the town. Matt knew that if the rain kept up, the road out to the Murchison River Gorge and the Hawks Head lookout would very quickly be impassable.

The rain softened a little. The dirt roads held. The little carpark at Hawks Head was completely deserted. We were soaked walking the hundred yards to the lookout. The river wound through a landscape utterly unacquainted with any form of human habitation or settlement: red dust and dry scrub made suddenly wet by the rains. Across the river we saw two feral goats high up in a cave.

We clambered down to the bend in the river where a pool formed. The gentle rain pocked the surface of the water with bubbles but made no sound. We stripped off our clothes and eased ourselves into the water from the mossy rocks. It was the first time we ever saw each other naked, outdoors. An obvious turning point in getting to know one another. I only felt a little shy. I noticed the red tinge in the black mass of his pubic hair, and the weird thought crossed my mind that, given my own genetic background, we would have red-haired children. I was getting ahead of myself. I dived fully into the water and swam through the murky green with my eyes wide open, trying not to think about crocodiles. When I burst back through the surface I turned and floated on my back; the sky was a bowl and I was its centre, so I was back in the moment and not thinking about genetics. Two birds flew overhead.

We had nothing to dry ourselves with. We drove back into Kalbarri in wet T-shirts and underwear. The Beach Boys sang about the girl who has fun in a T-Bird until her daddy takes the keys back off her when he realises she's been hanging around at the hamburger stand and not the library.

In the late afternoon Kalbarri was in the midst of a blackout. Buying candles at the local store, we learnt that so much dust settles on the power lines and the electricity plant during dry spells, that often at the first big rain the whole system shorts. The rain fell softly through the long dark evening. We tried to play backgammon by candlelight but the black pieces kept disappearing in the flickering shadows as if the dark bands of the board were doors that swallowed up the play. We lay on the couch and I played with Matt's toes as he told me more about his dreams for the management business.

'If Spud Gun works, I'm going to buy a house on the edge of the ocean,' he said.

Smiling in the dark, I pictured myself living in it.

The next day we slept in late and had lunch at the pub overlooking the bay. The clouds had lifted. We drove out the Red Bluff Road to the coastal gorges, past Madmans Rock and Goat Gulch to the Natural Bridge and Bluff Point. The whole continent sweeps flat and empty across the outback and the Great Western Desert then drops off suddenly at craggy cliffs into the ocean. The proposition that love, already nudged, would enter most readily into hearts made open and quiet by such vertiginous power in the glare of the sun, makes sense when I consider it now. So much else is a mystery, there are times it is hard to breathe. But I can say with certainty that, leaning against the safety barrier at the Bluff Point lookout, when I kissed him I knew I loved him.

It was the most languid of kisses and he groaned faintly. Below us along the curving cliff walls the swallows swooped and dived. The green sea heaved and the cliffs eroded, a pebble, a grain at a time. In a million years this would not be here. You seem to receive, on the edge of the ocean where the earth disappears, a sense of the size of the sky. I looked out across the Indian Ocean. Next stop Africa. Behind me there was an average population density of one person per ten square kilometres. I was glad not to be alone.

We walked hand in hand back to the car. From the scrubland we could hear the thrum of insects.

'Good, huh?' Matt smiled, and squeezed my hand. I was willing to go for the ride with this boy.

On the long stretch of beach just south of Kalbarri we went for a swim at the Blue Holes, a lagoon protected from the waves that broke on the reef a hundred metres further out. I was used to the grainy golden sand of Sydney's beaches, so the fine white sand like talc between my toes as I waded out was an odd sensation. At dusk we went to the fish-and-chip shop and took our hot parcel over the road to the park by the edge of the river, looking out to where it emptied into the ocean. The park was raucous with the delighted evening screechings of the pink and grey galahs and the white sulphur-crested cockatoos. They filled the trees and perched on the power lines and chased each other tumbling through the air. We would drive back to Geraldton in the morning. I would take the bus to Perth and the next day fly back to Sydney.

'I like you a lot,' I said.

'Is that all?' he said. 'I *really* like you.'

'No, "really" and "a lot" mean the same thing. I just said, "I like you a lot." That *means* "I really like you."'

'Okay then,' he said. 'In that case, I guess I really, *really* like you.'

'I really, really like you too, Matt,' I said, though at such points of embarkation, it seems that our words might be beside the point.

Matthew Smith

I WENT BACK TO SYDNEY, ALL MY NERVES TINGLING and Matt, the bringer of light, now looming so strongly in my life. Matt of the future, with eyes so blue they hurt you, all that dazzling reflection I'd seen back there on the islands. The way I'm trying to tell it seems exactly the way it was. Nothing is more correct than memory, in that once a lover is dead, it is the only version left. When Matt returned from the west a few weeks later it was as if we leapt right inside of each other.

In the early days, weeks, months, we were mostly interested in making love. I came to love his body more than any other I had known. And he, I guess, mine. What is love, in the beginning, if not this mapping out, this settling into the other's undulations?

With Matt things were different. When I made love with him it was the only time I did not feel disembodied. It was the only time it did not seem as if the actual act of sex was a high-speed struggle with flames, with something that could never be grasped. With Matt everything slowed down. I tasted his sweetness. I felt his body and we fitted together.

I came to realise, by way of contrast, that in the past when I had fucked other boys I had really been aware only of myself. When I made love with Matt I became suffused with an awareness of him. I became fascinated with every curve of muscle on his shoulder-blade, engrossed by the sweat on the arch of his neck when he came, hypnotised by the pounding of his heart against my hand.

Certain events stood out as we wove into each other's lives those threads of love. How he taught me to leap downwards, the opposite of the high jump. First you grow up and then you grow calmer.

Matt knew about a cliff twelve metres high on the harbour around from Watson's Bay. Now and then on summer weekends he jumped off this cliff with his friends. He somehow convinced me to jump, to swallow all that acrid adrenaline and leap from the edge. It was a rush of fear and relief but after the first jump I loved it. After a time I discovered that the fear began to go, and jumping off the cliff became for me like some weird act of meditation.

When I leapt out from the rock I experienced for that second of free fall a silence that enveloped me like a blanket. When I leapt I hung suspended in the air and the water came towards me and I heard nothing. As if controlled by a switch, all the ordinary sounds of the day dropped away instantly and there was nothing but the sun and the sky and the green water coming closer.

One weekday morning, though, we went there alone, and everything was different. I had always jumped in the afternoon, in the blazing sun, when the rocks were scattered with tribes of loud kids and all the air was light with noise.

Now I came with Matt on a dark morning, the air laden with heaviness and about to burst. The sky drizzled but the humidity was intense. Our shirts clung to our backs. A sweet and sticky aroma rose from the asphalt of the carpark where it had absorbed the thin soup of rain like a sponge.

We walked barefoot; only the sand on the path to the cliffs was cool. We were quiet that morning. This worked as a sign for me: a portent of love not because of silence itself but because that silence went in through my stomach before it registered anywhere else. I sensed a love so large I could travel vast distances and never once step outside it.

Even my heart that morning was not yet aware, could not have been aware, of an emotion that can be sensed only by some animal instinct, of a psychic rumbling not even the most delicate seismograph could trace.

The cliffs were deserted. We stood there alone, at 9 a.m. on a weekday in the rain, looking across the harbour at the city in the distance, and looking down to the green swell of water twelve metres below. He said then, with his hands plunged nonchalantly into his back pockets, that he loved me.

I sensed the warm grey morning crowding down, and in that unnatural summer gloom bridges of electricity flickered and sparked and fused between us. I had thought about it since Kalbarri but now, for the first time, I said the same words back to him. We kissed there on the cliff.

I had not known what kind of kiss it would be, short or long. At the last moment before contact our lips parted. We kissed for maybe three seconds, maybe five. It felt wet and hot, above all hot. We pulled away and I heard a faint murmur leave his lips; even so close, the sound was almost lost in the distance from his mouth to my ears. But it was there, distinct and clear, as if the whole world for that instant was that soft moan, that murmur of desire and melting—the murmur of all possibilities. I felt it in the spine, where it continued to echo and buzz.

He had to go to work: he had a meeting on behalf of Spud Gun, with a record company. We hadn't yet moved in together. That evening he turned up and we didn't even say a word. We kissed at the door of my bedroom and fell inwards onto the bed. He touched my breasts, which were tight and menstrual. I was filled with fluid. I rubbed my belly and groaned. My mind began to drift, deluged by the onslaught of wanting. We were becoming effortlessly unclothed. My nipples were erect, stretched tight in their expansion. My breathing was fast and shallow.

He said, 'I want to fuck you in the shower.'

I thought of all that effort. 'Fuck here.'

'No. You'll get blood on your sheets.'

'Blood? Blood is not a problem. Put it everywhere. We'll put a towel down.'

'Blood is fine. It's not that. But please, let's fuck in the shower. I want to do it on the hard floor. I don't know why. And the blood will wash away.'

I saw the look of dreaming and surrender in his eyes.

I felt beneath me the soft curves of the mattress and pillows and sheets. I thought of the sharp lines and right-angles of the tiles in the bathroom. I felt my legs go weak and light. A voice inside me said, 'The bathroom. The bathroom.' Clearly the bed would have been more comfortable, but sometimes comfort is not the point.

We left the light off in the bathroom. The steam from the shower could be seen framed in the patch of light that the window made. Only the moonlight shone through. A kind of sensory imbalance began to occur. The sticky heat engulfed us. The roar of the water seemed to echo exponentially on the tiles. It was an enormous old hot water boiler and the shower never ran out.

There was no other sound. But the sound of the water was everywhere. It was the same kind of silence and non-silence as on Big Rat Island.

In awkward positions, standing first and sliding downwards, we began to touch each other. He lowered me to the floor. The shower enclosure was as long as a bath and narrow. Our heads and shoulders were under the stream of water.

I heard nothing but that roar, felt nothing but heat. My thoughts began to warp in that sensory delirium. The thought flickered through my mind that I wished I had a machine to measure my skin temperature. What extraordinary level would it register? Everything went silver and wet and snapped into frantic overdrive, although everything happened in slow motion.

I knew nothing but water and skin: two-dimensional things. Then Matt entered me, and I began to drown in a three-dimensional world.

This is what happened. In that steamy darkness my eyelids fluttered. The colour all around was silver, the temperature close to scalding. The noise was deafening. My body felt weak and far away. We slid without friction in the wetness, in the water and the blood.

I manoeuvred around and lowered myself on top of him, his head tilted against the tiled wall, beneath the taps. I felt the hard spray of water hit the back of my head and stream through my hair and onto his face. We tried to kiss between gulps of water and gasps for air.

In the cramped space I raised my upper body away from him, arching my head back under the shower. With my arm around his neck I pulled him towards me. I held onto the soap dish for balance and pulled his face into my breasts. We moaned softly in rhythm, in surprise at such overwhelming pleasure.

We swayed for a while.

My eyes had adjusted a little. I saw his face faintly lit by the light from the window. All the world was liquid now, or else steam, liquid whose molecules have been agitated by heat.

My hair fell across his eyes. The water splashed in tiny silver splinters off his face. My eyes rolled upwards and I stared at absolutely nowhere, nothing, the dark far corners of the ceiling of the bathroom receding in the mists. I felt the first tug of momentum towards orgasm as one hears, in old movies, the distant whistle of the steam train. I began to rub myself to keep it on the rails. Round and round at the same time I thrust up and down on Matt.

As my pulse began to race I moaned almost soundlessly. Matt's lips parted a fraction more. A bridge of saliva stretched from his top to his bottom lip. It, too, was silver as it lengthened for an instant like elastic. A drop of water collided with the bridge and it exploded—I'm sure I heard the sound through the roar of the shower—with the minute hiss of liquid thrown on a hotplate.

I leant down for a moment to kiss his neck with an open mouth. His eyes were closed, his head flung sideways. I sat back up and watched him from a distance as I ground back and forth on the bone of his pelvis and felt him inside me. The more I arched the small of my back, the more I felt his belly against the fast-moving knuckles of my hand. I felt him start to come.

Then very suddenly, very powerfully, there came for me the moment of the freeze-frame—or was it strobing?—infinitely compressed, infinitely brief, infinitely extended, infinite. Physicists talk about the space-time foam, in which time does not move forward as elsewhere in the universe. Quantum theory says the space-time foam exists inside the 'naked singularity' of a black hole. The theory stresses the unknowability of the space-time foam state. And here it was, and is, beneath our noses.

During that moment there was no more sound, and there was nothing but infinite space, for a very long time, all around me. Even Matt was not there. All my muscles contracted. I pushed down on his cock, and shuddered, and rocked myself into an imploded place. Cradle and all. Then sound returned, and the noise of the echo of the water was like whole factories winding down, the whirring and spinning of gigantic wheels and cogs losing all momentum and drifting into a profound silence. And suddenly I was aware of my heart, as frantic as any voodoo drum.

We could hardly speak as we towelled ourselves. Well, it's hardly as if there was anything to say. We went to bed still slightly damp. He leant over and kissed me on each of my eyelids. We fell asleep deeply within minutes.

The real heart of love moved forward from there, the daily ups and downs, the big in the little event. Later, looking back, the day of the cliff and the night of the shower came to represent some mysterious point at which the way I looked at Matt began to change. Or perhaps I myself was beginning to change: ready for the thing to enter, and to enter into the thing; not the practice runs of the late teens and early twenties, but the heart in flood and the hard work too as life rolls on. Give it all to me, I thought I heard myself say.

The imaginatively named Matt Smith Management did indeed flower, and Spud Gun became, for a couple of years, one of the biggest bands in the country. He didn't get to buy or build his house on the cliff, but we lived near the beach at Bondi and were comfortable and happy. I set up a makeshift darkroom in the laundry and found a job in a photo lab. I was hoping to improve the developing techniques I had learnt in college. At this stage of my life I still clung, like many of my friends, to the romantic dream of being a photographer. Everything comes to nothing in the end, I suppose. Or at least, nothing happens exactly the way we imagine it.

Yet for several years we would work together through the good and the bad, the doubts and the bright certain moments, through all the long domestic haul and the tiny actions of the days. I came to realise that love was a series of such actions, and that action has a certain grace and power in it. All that I have told you is how the intertwining began. But life can be larger than love. I learnt too late, after four years of developing parallel loyalties and trust, permanence and commitment, leading up to talk of babies, that absolutely anything can happen and if it can it probably will. I learnt too late that what is most important to us is always most precious at the moment it occurs, and it is precious in its absolute immediacy and not as some vague confirmation of future directions; since the only certain fact, aside from death, is the flimsiness of everything. Such flimsiness hit me like a knockout blow in the photo lab, the day everything came to an end.

Accident

MATT'S DEATH SEEMED LIKE THE END OF MY LIFE, but in the strangest way it moved everything forward, to places like Paris and the place inside where you start to feel okay.

Tragedy arrived as a brutal interruption to the normal flow of time. It makes sense that there is a reservoir of time, possibly infinite but at least enormous, into which life dips; and then there is the time that flows, neither fast nor slow, in a landscape of pain. And there is never any way to prepare for the moment when you shift from the one to the other.

At the instant when I knew that he was dead, I was struck with horror by the fact that our last days together had been *particularly uneventful.* I'd been in the middle of the pleasantness of living my life and of being in a lasting relationship. After four years, and many ups and downs, we had seemed to be coming to a point of new commitment. Intimacy was a powerful thing.

It was an Indian summer. After the school year started again, the beach emptied out but the days remained warm. The light seemed to hang suspended hours beyond dusk. Matt's office was above a pub in Newtown and he was tour-managing overseas acts as well as managing Spud Gun and two other bands. We lived in North Bondi, away from the main traffic flow, in a desolate grid of streets that I had come to love. On sweltering afternoons when I wasn't working, Matt would ring sometimes and say he was leaving work early. He would make his way on his motorbike through the fumes of King Street and along Cleveland, and I would wait fifteen minutes then slowly amble to the north end of Bondi Beach, our meeting place. I would bring Matt's Speedos and an extra towel. We would while away a couple of hours, lying on our towels on the sand and chatting, going into the water whenever we got too hot.

The weather stayed balmy into early autumn. In Sydney, April is the loveliest month. One weekday afternoon we met. The sky was stretched tight like a lacquered drumskin. Instead of finding ourselves a space on the sand, we made our way past the children's pool and the rock pool and around the rocks of the north end to the fishermen's boat ramp near the point at Ben Buckler. We waited for a gap between waves and dived off the rocks into the deep water.

Later we ate laksa at the noodle bar on Campbell Parade. As the night came on I chatted on the phone to Louise while Matt worked on his motorbike under the porch light.

In the morning he was out of bed early; he had a big day on and wanted to beat the worst of the peak-hour traffic up Old South Head Road. He jumped in and out of the shower, made coffee and came into the bedroom.

'Okay, I'm off,' he said, setting my coffee down on the side table and kissing me on the forehead. 'What time do you finish today?'

'I work from ten till six.'

'Maybe we'll have a late swim, then?'

'Sure.'

'I'll ring you.'

'Okay.'

'Bye!'

'See you.'

A while later I got up and went to work in the photo lab. We mainly developed for magazines and publishers and professional photographers so it was always busy and I never had time to think. Matt hadn't rung by five o'clock and when I rang his office, the answering machine was on. 'Where are you?' I said. 'I'm leaving work soon.'

Fifteen minutes later I was in the darkroom developing the last print for the day. My mind was in neutral in the red womb of light, though I was vaguely aware of the anticipation, the pleasure that swimming in the ocean would bring. I always imagined the wash of photographic chemicals that clung to my skin during the course of work trailing behind me like a porpoise's wake as I dived beneath the waves for that first time.

There was a knock at the door. Sharon, the front-desk girl, called out. 'Uh, Isabelle, there's someone here to see you. I think it's urgent.'

'I'll be one minute.' I clipped a peg onto the last photo and rinsed the trays.

When I walked out into the foyer I was surprised—and happy—to see Matt's mother and father there. I smiled, then stopped. They were clutching each other, perched on the edge of the couch. Mrs Smith's face was white, her make-up streaked with tears.

'Hi Anne, hi Harvey…What? What is it?' And yet it was so clear it could only be one thing. Mrs Smith stood up and swept towards me and a half-strangled noise gurgled from her throat.

'Oh, Isabelle,' she moaned.

'Oh no,' I said softly.

'It's Matt.' She clasped my wrists. 'There's been an accident.'

'Is he okay?' It was a pure moment of change.

'He's dead,' she cried, and broke down completely. Mr Smith held her tight in his arms.

I turned away and gripped the counter. It is horrific how much these things are like movies. Did movies get it right or do they teach us how to act? Sharon was standing with her hands to her cheeks, her mouth open, her face white. Mr Smith, rigid with shock, was trying to soothe his wife. Inside of me one part was saying, 'There must be some mistake.' The other part, further away, but more insistent, was saying, 'That's it. Matt's gone. He is dead and everything's different.'

'An accident on King Street. Truck didn't see him,' Mr Smith said in a quavering voice, stroking his wife's hair, pulling me into a three-way hug. 'He was never conscious. Lived for an hour. We've identified the body. But if you need to see him too, we'll take you back there now.' The words were surreal. For as long as I'd known him he was Matt and now he was 'the body'. What did that mean? Was there a soul? It was inconceivable that we wouldn't meet again, the next day, perhaps, at the beach, when all of this was over.

'Yes. Oh yes,' I said. 'We have to go there now.'

We drove to the hospital, Mr Smith driving, Mrs Smith and I clutching each other in the back seat. I gazed numbly out of the window and watched the faces of the people passing in the street. Most had been touched by death. Everyone was marked by it.

When we arrived we found that the body had already been taken to the morgue. I was gliding through the passive heat of shock and so nothing came as an inconvenience.

The morgue was, like the hospital, a world of antiseptic smells, hard lines and linoleum floors, and yet it lacked the hospital's manic urgency, was devoid of bustle: a place where hope and fear were making the transition into defeat and acceptance.

I was trembling as the doctor led me into the coolroom. Again, I was so entirely prepared for this event: everything was exactly as I'd seen it in the movies. Matt lay on a metal trolley in the middle of the room. A grey sheet covered his body. The doctor pulled it back and stood aside. There lay a whole huge swathe of my future, babies and travel and dreams and a long life together.

Matt was as handsome as always but the life that was him was not there. His lips were a pale purple and his face a deathly talcum-white, as if made up for a party joke. I touched his cheeks softly with my fingertips, the lightest of grazes already weighed down by the nostalgia of years ahead. He had never made it to work that morning. The image of his face disappeared behind the tears I couldn't blink out of my eyes, so endlessly and soundlessly were they falling. I felt a sense of desperation; it was the last time I would ever see Matt, and he was distorted, like I was looking at him from behind a waterfall. I stepped aside, blew my nose and wiped my eyes, and tried to force myself to stop crying. 'Later,' I said to myself. 'There'll be enough time to cry.' The doctor moved a half-step, ready to pull the sheet back across.

Wait, I motioned with my hand. 'Can you pull the sheet down further, please?'

He undraped the sheet to Matt's waist. Matt had taken the full force of the truck's fender side-on and in the torso,

I would learn later. Though welts could be seen where his arm had been broken in several places, the skin was not marked but for slight contusions and abrasions. He died from massive internal haemorrhaging, and the faint bands of purple on his chest and stomach were no more than the surface residue of the profound catastrophe that had mangled his insides and ended his life. It is simply terrible, the frailty of the human body.

I looked at his face for one last time. I looked at the doctor: a clear, clean face, young and strong, that I would always remember.

'Thank you,' I whispered.

He pulled the sheet up and Matt was gone.

I walked back outside to Mr and Mrs Smith in the waiting room. They stood up expectantly and before I could reach them I fainted. My mind tries to hold the scene together. That is pretty much all I remember from that day.

≋ *News in Brief*

FOR A LONG TIME I CARRIED THIS CLIPPING IN MY PURSE, as if it were the thing that made Matt's memory immortal. When I realised the folly of such a bearing, as I read it for the umpteenth time, perhaps on the Paris metro, perhaps in the Jardin du Luxembourg, I crumpled it and threw it away. It was a decisive moment in establishing forward momentum. But I see no reason—at any rate, it's on the microfiche forever—not to record it here.

Sydney Telegraph-Mirror, 11 April 1997

MOTORCYCLIST DIES

A motorcyclist was killed on King Street, Newtown, yesterday morning when his bike and a truck collided. West-bound traffic was delayed for more than an hour.

The dead man is Matthew Anthony Smith, 31, of Bondi. Police have interviewed a 45-year-old truck driver from Picton. A police spokesperson said last night it was likely that charges of negligent driving and failing to stop at a give-way sign would be laid against the driver.

After Matt

AFTER MATT DIES THERE ARE BRIEF MOMENTS IN THE long haul of months when I feel that there might come a time when everything will fit into place and I will accept Matt's death as a part of my life. That he's out of my life, for some bizarre reason ordained by the greater forces, so that the way can unfold and the life can truly begin. Death makes you think that cosmic stuff. Loss makes you focus on it, maybe too much. I watch the shadows on the terrace creep through the afternoon. Matt is like a ghost and for a moment all the pain is gone. Imperceptibly, more time passes when I'm not remembering our every moment together, not recreating our every conversation, re-imagining our love-making. It is immeasurably sad.

My consciousness of these moments of relief from the thought of Matt comes to me as a shock. I will think, with some delight, I've just spent four minutes enjoying myself. How did that happen?

Two weeks after the funeral I call Matt's mother and say, 'It's just too painful, Anne. So many of his things are everywhere. This is hard, but I think it's a good idea if we pack some stuff away or give it away. If you and Harvey came and got some stuff. Or maybe the boys might want to take some things.'

The whole family, Anne and Harvey and Matt's three brothers, come over one sad Saturday. Matt's life is divided into throw-away piles and 'put in the van' piles. Peter takes the surfboard. I keep the stereo. The two older brothers manage some feeble laughs at Matt's CDs—'I don't know who any of these bands are,' says David, 'but I can tell by the covers that it's not my kind of music.'

'We can divide them,' I say to Peter.

I keep most of Matt's small collection of books. Lots of poetry, some that I'd bought him. Matt always claimed Robert Louis Stevenson's *A Child's Garden of Verse* was the greatest poetry ever written. Who am I to argue? It's a profoundly beautiful book. I'd found it in a junk shop, a turn-of-the-century copy for a dollar. 'To Matt—in the garden, the thicket, the jungle—wherever! Happy birthday and love always, Isabelle.' The boys divide the clothes they like and the rest are marked for the Salvation Army collection bin.

Mrs Smith stands looking out the window and begins to cry. David and Peter try to comfort her. She points to the pile of clothes on the floor.

'It's just,' she says, 'it's just…It seems such a silly little bundle of things to show for a life.'

I remember the dirty washing that has remained in the laundry, untouched since the funeral. I go in and stare at the glum grey pile for a moment, then force myself to bend down and sift out Matt's clothes. I pick from the pile his favourite T-shirt: blue, with the NASA logo. I press it to my face, breathe deep. A hot flush courses through me. I throw the T-shirt into the corner.

I gather up the rest of his clothes and take them back out to the living room. As opposed to the dead room. When Anne and Harvey and the boys all drive away in their separate cars, I know there will be less and less reason to see them and that eventually, it is possible, there will be little or no contact.

One night, a month or two later, a black thunderstorm rages through Sydney: normally a reason for the skin to tingle with excitement. But tonight the whipping of raindrops on the windowpane frightens and depresses me and I feel a shivering in my bones. I see a vision of myself as a ghost; as a great white canvas sail on a four-master ship. It is frayed and tattered as the gale lashes it. Finally it disintegrates into shreds carried off into the night on Force 10 winds.

It's ten o'clock. I ring Father Sheehy, the priest who officiated at the funeral and who had said, and meant it, 'Ring me any time you need to talk. It's good to talk sometimes.'

'My dear darling Isabelle,' he says. 'No, of course it's not too late. I've thought about you a lot. Above all, your courage.'

But I don't feel I have any. It's just that a decent priest can know the right words. And know how to listen. I talk and talk and barely have a clue what I'm saying. I talk, it seems, for months—to my mother, to my friends, to Louise in particular. And everything, I know, is a part of some great outpouring of Matt, all of the Matt that had gone into me over four years and rested there as part of me, just as part of me had gone into Matt and had left with him, wrenched away from my own self, when he died. I know that for months I have been like a vast cup pouring itself out, a steady flow of Mattness that is not, viewed logically, endless, but certainly feels so in the heart.

I believe the old saying, 'If it's not practical, it's not spiritual.' But what I want to hear tonight is impractical advice of the highest order.

Father Sheehy, a down-to-earth man, says many kind things. Finally I blow my nose and say, 'Father, I know it's late. I'm going to go now.'

'Remember,' he says, 'it's written in the Bible—goodness gracious me, I've forgotten exactly where!—well, never mind. *Somewhere* in the Bible, it says that God is in the hearts of those who suffer and who hope. Think about it, Isabelle. It's extraordinary. It's beautiful. God is in the hearts of those who suffer and who hope.'

God can go to hell, I think. Where was He for Matt?

'So through all this,' Father Sheehy continues, 'God, how ever you choose to conceive of God, is in your heart too. That's all that faith is, Isabelle. The knowledge that the greater thing is with you. That's all the faith you need. The knowledge that you are not the greater thing.'

When the storm has abated the next day I walk down to the beach. I take a long stroll along the path that leads around the rocks and south towards Coogee. I walk as far as the cemetery at Bronte. Down to my left the ocean swell lumbers in and explodes upon the rocks. Above me to the right, the hill is jam-packed with the headstones that have the best ocean views in Sydney. The salt-swept cemetery is a beautiful place. Today it is simply bleak.

I walk back the way I came, through Bronte Beach and the rocks at McKenzies Bay. On a flat rock just off the path is an Aboriginal carving of a whale, rarely noticed by the passers-by. It is thousands of years old. And yet all I want is the hot breath of Matt on my neck, in my ear, the urgency of my fumbling at the buttons of his shirt.

The sky swirls with fast-moving dirty grey clouds, the remnants of the storm. There is a chill in the air. I come to the Bondi promenade and walk down the ramp onto the beach. I take off my shoes and the sand is cold. The high tide line is littered with piles of kelp. A brown stain of foam marks the flat hard sand near the water. The sea is dirty with debris and the small waves bunch, choppy and angry. Nobody is swimming or surfing.

I idle my way along the length of the beach and climb the steps at the north end, back onto the promenade. It's a quiet day for Bondi: mid-week, blustery weather. I sit on one of the benches facing south, the way I have just come. The afternoon sun, when it appears through the scudding clouds, warms my face.

In the distance I notice an elderly woman walk down the ramp in front of the surf-lifesaving building and across the sand towards the children's bathing pool. The woman wears no shoes and I imagine she has left them in her car. She hitches her dress a little and steps knee-deep into the edge of the ocean. Then she moves towards the bathing pool and disappears momentarily, out of view beneath the ledge and the wooden railings against which a jogger stretches.

I doze with my eyes open, lulled into the trance that Bondi, empty of crowds and open to ocean and sky, can induce. The clouds race low across the sky and disappear towards Rose Bay as if late for an appointment. They are thin clouds now, becoming sparser; sitting sheltered at the sunny end of the promenade, my skin warms and I take off my coat.

I watch a man come down the ramp with his daughter, a tiny hyperactive girl. He's laden down with a plastic bucket and spade and towels and a carry bag. It's obvious from a distance who's the boss and who's organised the trip to the beach, despite the weather and against all odds. I smile. The little girl's thin voice carries broken and fragmented on the wind, ordering her father to hurry up. Then they too disappear from view, in the direction of the children's pool.

Always, everywhere, the world is filled with collisions.

I let the sounds flow through me. The squawking of seagulls approaches and recedes as they make their squabbling rounds. Fragments of conversation reach me from the occasional couple walking past. 'I know, I know. It's dreadful,' I hear. And later, from two women pushing prams: 'I could have rung Malcolm, but it was meant to be a surprise.' A car horn blares on Ramsgate Avenue. Further along the beach two men begin hitting a squash ball to each other with paddle bats; the *pock* of ball on bat is a sharp clear sound through the swishing of the wind and reaches me out of sync with the movements of their arms.

Behind all the other sounds is the one I love the most: the endless echoing of the ocean. It is as if the cells inside my body recognise the breaking of the waves and their hissing onto the sand from some time long ago.

I hear a woman's rough and raucous shouting, but as always at North Bondi, it's difficult to tell from which direction the noise is coming. Then the words become clear as I strain my ears.

'You keep away from her!' the voice is screaming.

There is a lower voice in reply, the voice of a man, but the words are indistinct.

'Don't you touch her! You keep away from her! I saw what you were doing!'

And again, the indistinct voice replies, more aggressive this time.

I realise it's coming from the children's pool. Curiosity being far stronger than discretion, I walk over to the railing and look down. It's the barefoot woman and the man with his daughter. The woman is standing at the far side of the pool in its deepest part, up to her thighs. Her hitched-up dress is wet where it has dipped into the water; her thighs are dimpled. The man is standing below me. The daughter, with spade in hand, is beginning to cry.

'Who is she, Daddy?' She cowers behind her father's leg. He tries to stroke her hair and maintain a threatening attitude to the woman at the same time. 'She's just a silly old lady, darling. You're a stupid old woman!'

Impervious, the woman points. 'You leave her alone! You leave her alone!'

The father steps into the wading pool. Unbelievably, the woman steps towards him.

'You stupid old woman, you're scaring my daughter. How dare you!'

She points again, arm outstretched, and continues to wade towards him. 'You leave her alone! I saw what you did!'

Crouching on the sand, the little girl starts to tremble and blubber. The man retreats and starts gathering their things. 'Don't you worry about her,' he says to his daughter. 'She's just a stupid old woman. Come on, we'll go find somewhere else to play.'

The woman stands where the man had been a moment before. 'You leave her alone!' she screams.

'Look, this is beyond a joke, woman. Look at what you're doing to my daughter. Now go away!' He flings his arm towards her.

She takes another step closer. 'Leave her alone!'

The man steps out into the water and gives the woman a hard shove. 'Get out of here!' he shouts.

She loses her balance and falls backwards into a squat. Her dress billows out from her. The man turns and goes to his daughter. The things he had arrived with, so neatly packed, are in disarray. He tries to gather everything up in a hurry but the plastic bucket or one of his sandals or a towel keeps falling to the sand. He leaves them where they fall.

The woman changes tack. 'Come and play with me, little girl!' She keeps abreast of them as they move up the sand. I am trying to move through the months after Matt by finding positive things to focus on, but it seems that I am drawn to this ugliness that lurks beneath the surface of everything, ready to erupt.

'Come and play with me, little girl! Come and play with me, little girl!' The woman's voice is hoarse from shouting, manic. There on the sand on the wind-blown day, she truly seems the hag with the gingerbread cottage, the witch who boils children's heads into soup. The little girl is hysterical.

Everybody's breathless. It's primal. 'Come and play with me, little girl!'

'Right, I'm calling the police,' the father shouts as he moves up the ramp.

The woman stands in the sand. 'Daddy loves you!' she's shouting, her voice hysterical. 'Daddy loves you, little girl! Daddy loves you! Daddy loves you!'

The father and daughter drive away, the daughter sobbing. It's all over; nobody else seems to have noticed. The woman wanders back to the water, muttering to herself. Everybody is locked in their own agony and palpitations and the hot flush of blood that courses faster than events.

She enters the water. For a moment I wonder about her intentions, whether I'll be forced to dive in after her. It is high tide so the waves are breaking where the sand is steep and the old woman is waist-deep only a few steps in. Her dress floats around her like the soft translucent hood of a jellyfish. She seems happy now. She splashes around, her movements childlike. She never submerges herself but follows the line of the shore as she moves towards the southern end. She is frolicking, splashing, pirouetting. It's a little bit unusual, a woman in a dress moving along like that a few metres offshore, but it's not, at Bondi, radically unusual. In the reflected glare and the salt haze, you can barely make her out.

She takes her time. In half an hour she has not even travelled half the length of the beach. I wonder where she lives, where she came from today, why she is at Bondi, how often she gets hospitalised. The whole event is gone, just like that, and leaves only a trace of its sadness, and after a while she shimmers and disappears altogether into the glare of the setting sun.

Matthew himself is nothing if not an evaporation. If we could love more fully, knowing that all is going away, we would indeed be lucky. But the wind is howling and clutters our thoughts. Immobile on the bench, I wish for my own tender heart to cease to beat. What in the world is it that makes everything continue?

PART

Two

The other phrase that comes to mind is more obscure. It is the Latin motto from the title banner of the *North Georgia Gazette: per freta hactenus negata,* meaning to have negotiated a strait the very existence of which has been denied. But it also suggests a continuing movement through unknown waters.

BARRY LOPEZ

Arctic Dreams: Imagination and Desire in a Northern Landscape

Baxter, Victim of Powerful Forces, and Other Boys

AFTER MATT'S DEATH, THE BLANKNESS OF IT ALL, THE dividing of the worldly goods, the awful sadness of the old lady on the beach, there is for many months the feeling of wading through treacle. I remove myself from family and friends. I take time off from the photo lab. I watch daytime television. There is *Days of Our Lives*, which will keep screening long after the sun exhausts its fuel and fries the planets in its death throes. There is newer American fare, the hypnotically bad, confessional talk shows. On *The Ricki Lake Show* a red-faced audience member stabs the air with her finger and shouts at a guest: 'You're stuck on stupid, Victor, waiting to get dumber!'

On the ABC I watch a documentary about trout. I'm sure the trout, both species and individual, must be happy, but not in any way we can imagine.

I am trying to claw my way back into the world, though probably a little handicapped by Louise's hydroponic home-grown crop. We deal with things as best we can. When I'm not watching TV I'm devouring books. And they all seem to be about Death. Of course, I want to be in tune with the greater universe.

In the strange moments before sleep, where all control is illusion, I see flickering images of a world of men with elongated foreheads: not the evolutionary result of the brain growing ever larger and more complex, but bony protrusions for headbutting during the rutting season. I see women with transparent skin and veins that flush different colours to give different signals.

The hydroponics bends me a little. Alone, ABC again, I watch cuttlefish mate on another documentary. Where do all the fish come from? Television loves them. At the moment when the male deposits sperm into the body of the female, his tentacles wrap around hers. In the split second of coupling, his body changes colour from white or grey to a vivid pulsing crimson. The narrator tells us that this is so other males know what is taking place and keep away.

In the violent flush of colour down the body of the cuttlefish, in that radical seizure of reddening, I see a parallel and know that I have had in my own life moments of such primary singularity. When will they come again? I know a moment approaching orgasm when thought and emotion are stripped of all structure and form in a change as pervasive as the chromatic thermonuclear pulse of a cuttlefish coupling. I know that the mind enters a state as primal as a blind fish fucking on the ocean's crowded floor.

At other moments a lightness has filled my body until it seems to have no mass. My consciousness is nothing but equations. I hurtle through graphs in four dimensions; an exquisite wind careens through my head, until at last I feel all my being contracted into a weightless point somewhere deep in the pit of my gut. And in such a state of abstraction I feel connected for an instant to the world. Where in fact, I try to remind myself, I live. And yet all I miss is Matt: something as simple as his boiling the jug for the tea.

At any rate, despite how good documentaries can be, TV is hit or miss, not such a good thing when you're feeling depressed. It is the comedy section of VideoPlus, far more even than Louise's giggly dope, that helps sees me through the worst of the treacle time. And all those thoughts of sex? For four months, maybe five, I remain absolutely alone. It would be impossible to see someone else.

One day an insurance company tracks me down: they have a juicy cheque for me, Matt's life insurance. He had named me as the sole beneficiary. I had no idea he'd even taken a policy out. I am frightened—it is as if I have received a gift from the dead—but at the same time I take it as a sign from the heavens to move a little faster into my future. I stop smoking the hydro. I start to think about travel. I figure if I go back to the lab, increase my shifts, work hard for a few months, save all my money and put it together with the cheque, I might last a year or more overseas. Try to put Matt behind me, move on. Everything about falling in love with Matt reminds me of the ocean. I decide I must go far away from the ocean for a while. But it must be to a beautiful place. I have always dreamt of Paris. Well, we've all seen the photos.

I work like a maniac; the money begins to build up. I go to French classes three nights a week. Some of the high-school basics come back to me.

In the meantime I go back at last to clubs and pubs to see bands with Louise and our friends. There are times I nurse my sorrow as if it were a polished stone that I finger deep in my pocket. But on loud nights of raw thrash and guitar fuzz, there are times I forget myself again, as I did when I was nineteen and my father went to prison.

On such a night of lightness and buoyancy I meet Baxter at a club. We dance and go back to my place. He is tall and gangly with dredlocks beginning to sprout in his hair and thick horn-rimmed glasses like some intellectual DJ. We roll together lazily on my bed. It's been easy to drink too much vodka on such a warm night. We waver on the fine line between falling asleep and fucking, but begin to head towards the latter.

It's late in the night and a light rain falls. We kiss. I suck his fingers. The smell of my own mid-cycle coupled with the newness of the Baxter smell makes me so horny my toes are tingling and the smell of summer rain on the asphalt outside makes me feel that I live once again, or at least for these moments, in a benign universe. Baxter seems to know approximately what to do with his tongue. I am exactly where I was always meant to be, in the right place and at the right time.

We make love in the missionary position. Baxter takes his weight off me and raises himself up with his arms, supporting himself on his knees. He moves in and out of me slowly. It's really very nice and I moan a little. He takes my hand and guides it down my belly. I start to rub my clitoris lightly and gradually my hand moves faster.

As I continue to rub myself I begin to notice that the knuckle at the base of my middle finger is grazing Baxter's pelvic bone. At first this seems only to be part of the incidental body contact of sex. But gradually I become more and more aware of the tiny circle of delicate repetitive pressure I make on his skin, and my mind begins to focus in on it and nothing else. It is good to be alive, knuckle bone and pelvic plate tapping at each other like that.

At 4 a.m. the rain lets loose in deafening torrents. Not only good to be alive, but nice to come with a stranger. Intimacy? For now I want nothing of it. I am simply trying to emerge from the violent unnecessariness of death.

Things begin to flow from one boy to another. I am full of nervous tension. What am I grasping at here? Well, it is all such a blur, so hard to describe. Like nothing I have known before or since. It might be six months or more but it seems only like several weeks.

Very quickly I begin to understand the selfishness of my love, the inappropriateness of my relationships, when I realise that every time I fuck it feels as if I am wrestling with demons.

My series of transient lovers feel this too. They develop a compelling curiosity about my plight, and each hangs around for a couple of weeks. Sooner rather than later they sense the inviolability of the wall that surrounds me. Then they leave. If they don't jump I push them. I am trying to get from one place to another: start here, go through this, get there, put Matt to rest. Will it ever work? At any rate, for a while they are fascinated to be the medium through which some demented struggle takes place.

In the act itself there is a point at which a light that comes from nowhere starts flickering like a strobe. What happens is not exactly a hallucination. But it wells up from deep in the earth and pounds through my body and there is nowhere to escape from its intensity.

We writhe together as if in liquid. We are vaguely humanoid. Thunder explodes in the ears and then thought is not possible.

A while later the body returns.

Coming out of that state, I carry with me the distant memory of a metamorphic experience. A vague sense of some fundamental molecular change infuses my lovers too, but this sense never solidifies into concrete thought for them. With sex, most men are going through the motions. They are not in tune with the poetry or the physics of the thing. They feel my frantic grasping, my thrusting against them, as a physical action in time and space. Meanwhile I am aware only of electrical fields and gigantic solar flares in front of my eyes. Even with my eyes open, in the middle of making love, the solar flares pulse so that I might be blind, engulfed in all light.

And afterwards, sadness. I can hardly share it with these men; I was taught by wonderful parents that cruelty is inexcusable. I do not understand what force spreads my mind so thinly through each pore of my body. I understand only that a vast void, an emptiness, is needing to be filled. O the things we grasp at.

One day all this takes place at dusk. His name is Jimmy but I call him, inside my head, Baxter Two. I seem to be settling into type. The sky is humid, the afternoon sticky. Baxter Two's tumbledown house in the back of Erskineville perches amidst the renovated weatherboard cottages like a hamburger at a Chinese feast. All summer it feels as if it will rain soon. All summer the strange feeling, 'something will break.'

We've been seeing each other, on and off, for a month or so. I guess we like each other about the same. Moderate interest. I met him at a party and we got on fine. For a while the absolute focus and meditative calm with which he tinkers with the various cars that appear, as if from nowhere, in his driveway seems to me the sexiest thing

I can imagine. But soon enough that fantasy fades and Baxter Two becomes just another nice boy, slightly distracted, smoking his bongs. I am keen to see him whenever he turns up but I lack any specific concept of our place in the scheme of things. He looks enough like an outsider, someone to assuage the pain. But I talk about calling it quits. 'Let's wrap things up before they begin,' I say. It's been pleasant enough; the truth is, I don't seem just now to be able to engage my emotions into a gear.

Later Baxter Two says, 'I'll remember little things.'

'Little things,' I say. 'That's what the world's made up of.'

'If this is going to end,' continues Baxter Two, 'I won't want to see you at all. You're beautiful, but you're somewhere else. That's okay. I can handle that. But we won't continue as friends, not just now. I like you as a lover, not a friend.'

'I understand that,' I say.

At the door, leaving, I say, 'Well...'

Baxter Two says, 'Well...see you.'

I walk to my car feeling light-headed. It's still humid at midnight. Bats fly overhead.

Three days later I bump into him again, on the crowded street in sweltering Newtown. His eyes are huge and black. I think about desire. There are flickerings that occur, and we know very little about them. Millimetres of dilation are words in a language. But we talk for a couple of minutes and then go off in different directions.

I want the light I feel for him—for any boy, perhaps—to glow white hot. It's a light inside my head. And yet

I know clearly, somehow, that when the time is not right there is nothing in the world I can do to push things; there is nothing for it but to sit through all the discomfort, obeying a timetable not my own. These boys are like some giant distraction. And then it strikes me that patience is the most difficult thing in the world.

All that matters is memory, and all I have is a rose-tinted Matt of motorbikes and loud thrash bands, summers of sex, warm winters, something that felt like direction. And now, with Baxter One, or Two, whoever, an endless and intense energy directed at nothing. Something to pass the time. Matt's death represents very little that could be construed as being positive. But out of it comes, for this brief and troubling time, the liberty with which I can selfishly and without guilt explore that strange thing (sex, desire, the intermeshment of it all) that burns inside me. And even that doesn't work. Why am I jumping out of my skin like this?

I know I know nothing of the future. I know I know nothing of hope. When I look at the present I see it is only my body that is hot. The faint embers of warmth in my desperate couplings are enough, almost, to ward off the cold tang of the weeks and the months.

And then I know it's time to leave, bang, just like that. My money is itching to go. What else is it for, I think, if not to liquefy our most frozen yearnings? Money: congealed energy. It is time to stop with the dance of replaceable boys. Time to get rid of all traces of the life I'd planned, in order to make room for the life that might be waiting for me. I think more and more now of elsewheres. At last I board the plane that will take me a hemisphere away from the past.

If it's true that time can heal, as it slowly does, then geography might speed things up even more. I fly north around the globe, to Paris, which for everyone other than Parisians is the city of all myth: Paris, where the particles of light that cling to travellers the world over come to rest, come to earth, and settle into the very contours of the footpaths.

Birds That Are Fish of the Sky

I TRY TO READ PARIS AS A POEM, SINCE POSSIBLY ONLY poetry can redeem us from decay. Loss and decay: I'd become familiar with these things. In Paris I am cut so far adrift from everything I've ever known that I feel, deep in the part of the brain that controls balance, nearly imperceptible shifts in the ground beneath my feet, so that the city becomes an enormous ship lumbering stately and serene through an ocean vast beyond imagining.

In Paris I begin to walk. There is so much tension that death puts in our shoulders. With walking comes breathing. As I sigh the whole of Paris sighs. The city, in fact, is nothing but a series of emanations, exhalations softer than dawn, which drape themselves over the skin and sink into its pores like the faintest of dews.

I develop an 'algorithm of wandering': a simple system that gives structure to the days. I walk along a given street or boulevard; after a while the thought might enter my head to change direction. At the very next intersection I must head left, or right, or continue straight ahead, according to where the most light comes from. I walk the streets for hours, whole mornings, whole afternoons.

I feel that a great unknownness has descended all around me. The ship called Paris in a sea of unfathomable beauty. I begin to feel through all the sadness a gratitude for being alive that is like a small child constantly tugging at my sleeve. Possibly it can lead me to the places of its desire. Gratitude. I have no desires of my own.

I arrive in early spring—nearly a year since Matt died—when the city has barely begun to wake from the winter freeze. I wear a scarf wherever I go. After a couple of false starts I find a furnished bedsit to rent, off Rue St Jacques, up on the south edge of the Latin Quarter, and I settle in. I have a bed and a desk, a lion-foot bath, a basic kitchen. It is a den, a cocoon from which to explore, to which I can retreat.

I discover the river Seine at dusk. I had thought that pleasure was accidental and not something that can be located in the same place every day.

For some weeks I walk to the river every evening, timing my strolls to arrive about half an hour before sunset. I walk down Rue St Jacques to arrive at the Petit Pont across the square from Notre Dame. From there I walk west along the river towards the setting sun. From this point in the journey there are eleven bridges to explore before I arrive, within an hour, at the Eiffel Tower. By then it is generally dark. Should I begin the journey earlier, and continue past the Eiffel Tower, there are another four bridges before the Boulevard Périphérique crosses the river near the heliport at the bottom of the Sixteenth arrondissement.

These last four bridges include the Pont Mirabeau, which the poet Apollinaire immortalised. Matt had loved Apollinaire. Standing on the bridge one time, looking down at the water, I begin to cry. I remember how I'd been so surprised to meet a deckhand who liked poetry. When the sun has dipped over the horizon I ask a man crossing the bridge to take my photo. I have been looking at this photo, pinned to the wall in front of me, the whole time I have been writing this story, my story. I am wrapped up warm and cosy on the right-hand side of the photo, that weak, shy smile brought on by the self-consciousness of smiling at a stranger on a bridge as the traffic of Paris flows by. The bright orange sky seeming to envelop me. Beside this photo, another one: Matt, on Terry Breen's boat, off the Western Australian coast, the sun in his eyes.

As my French gets better I try to translate Apollinaire's poem into prose that makes some basic sense to me. Matt had once given me a slim volume by Wallace Stevens, explaining that reading poetry—reading Stevens in particular—was good for dislodging 'the stuck bits in the brain.' I hadn't read Stevens at that time, so there's yet another thing to thank Matt for eternally. Maybe translating poetry, more so than reading it, could do some similar act of dislodging. Those stuck bits in the spirit too.

I decide to attempt the translation to honour the memory of the Matt I loved, who is fading. *The Seine flows under the Mirabeau Bridge, as does our love. Why does it have to remind me of that? Joy always came after pain. May the night arrive. May the hour strike. The days go by. I remain standing here. Hands in hands, let us stay face to face, while eternal glances pass under the bridge made by our arms. The little waves so weary. May the night arrive. May the hour strike. The days go by. I remain standing here. Love slides past like this flowing water. Love goes away. But oh how slow is life and how violent is hope. May the night arrive. May the hour strike. The days go by. I remain standing here. The days pass and the weeks pass. But neither the past nor all that was our love can come back. The Seine flows under the Mirabeau Bridge. May the night arrive. May the hour strike. The days go by. I remain standing here.*

Poetry and photography: I have entered the noble causes. One is immeasurably old, the deepest magic, the other so new it is still a transparent magic. Everywhere I go I take photos. It's not that photography recaptures the world you have been in; more that it creates a new one: photographs are like Post-It Notes reminding us of the deep architectonic forms of space and thought. Eventually I will come back to Sydney with more than a thousand photos, of which less than fifty will resemble anything like tourist snaps. The others are all doorways, the grains of woods, the green foundry-work of old lampposts, edges of zebra crossings on cobblestones, lace metalwork of the grilles surrounding trees in parks, pebbles on the paths in the Luxembourg Gardens, rainbows trapped in the breezes from fountains, stone walls. Marblings and grains, ruffles and whorls in the make-up of things, the unseen lineaments of daydream. The lintels of windows, where one might see, forgotten by time, forgotten by the city, in a shaft of sunlight, there where the wood has weathered and cracked and the paint flaked away, the delicate fuzz of a spider's web in the corner. Eventually the best couple of hundred of these photos will go into a book I make, an album really, limited edition of one copy, called *The Textures of Paris* by Isabelle Airly. It will be Louise's thirtieth birthday present, and she will hug me and kiss me for it.

I walk and walk. In the other direction from the Petit Pont, on the Right Bank side of the Ile de la Cité and the Ile St Louis, there are seven other bridges to explore, as well as the Pont St Louis which joins the two islands. After my early haphazard explorations of all the bridges, I decide to walk out each day on a series of expeditions, each in honour of the contemplation of a different bridge. For the Seine, I see, is a rupture in the heart of Paris, and the bridges are the sutures that bind it back together.

I start my new journeys at the Pont St Louis. The tiny bridge is closed to cars. On weekends it is crowded with buskers—bad clowns usually, breathing fire or juggling tenpins for the tourists—but today it's a grey Tuesday and I'm pleased by the emptiness. In certain light before storms the grey slate roof of the Hotel de Ville across the water takes on a steel-blue sheen bordering on bruised purple. The statues on its roof turn pale, fading green against the austere sky. Further in the distance is the medieval Tour St Jacques, brooding and ominous, so mundane at the base, rising up to the magnificent asymmetry of its gargoyles, as if the tower were built solely for the purpose of repelling the attacks of airborne demons. My eyes wander along the old stone apartment buildings that line the Quai aux Fleurs and I wonder what kind of people are living in them. The flower dock. Rich people, I guess.

If you relax enough you can see things that aren't there any more. In Paris, my cortex seems to be opening to a luminescent universe. What I initially think are some kind of hallucinations—worrying term—I come to realise are instead this more relaxed way of seeing.

So it is no surprise when the stone river walls and the footpaths of the Quai aux Fleurs take on a sudden sunburst of colour and there before me, layer upon layer, is every flower ever unloaded from a barge. A thousand years of flowers, finishing their journey from the rich soil upriver. The flowers burst the seams of the atmosphere, spilling over each other in cascading torrents until finally my eye can take in nothing more than chaotic arrangements of colour, and I blink hard, and the chaos goes.

I watch the water. A school of debris floats by. A white shopping bag drifting aimlessly reminds me of Sydney, of the jellyfish that float around the ferries at Circular Quay. The same formlessness, a transparent membrane. Then the first drops of rain begin to fall and I hurry home.

I love the river, and all the bridges. But I miss the ocean: that feeling of well-being that comes after a winter swim at Bondi, the salty skin tingling. Back at my apartment, as the storm opens out and lashes the bamboo and the tiger lilies on my terrace, I run a bath and throw in handfuls of sea salt from the kitchen, thinking that perhaps I can trick the cells in my body into believing they have taken that plunge into pleasure. The afternoon turns dark from the low clouds. I turn the radio on softly and light a candle in the bathroom before sinking into my mini-ocean. It doesn't feel like Bondi, of course, but the music and the water relax me so much that I realise what I miss, yet again, is Matthew Smith. I don't cry so much these days but in a salty bath on a dark day huge exceptions can be made. I thought I was getting better some time ago; maybe it was only hydroponic hooch and temporary Baxters. You've got to watch out for those screens and illusions. Sometimes there is nothing for it but to batten down the hatches at the same time you open the floodgates. At all times Time makes all the rules, and like the Buddha said—or more

likely the Brahma, pacing out his godly billions of aeons—
'Impatience is the only sin.'

The spring days lengthen; it's around the central cluster of bridges, and heading a little west, about as far as the
Pont Royal or the Pont Solferino opposite the Garden of
the Tuileries, where I spend most of my time on my dusk
adventures. I like to linger on the cast-iron Pont des Arts,
which leads across the river to the main courtyard of
the Louvre. It's a wooden-planked pedestrian bridge with
benches running along the middle; beneath it the tourist
barges ply their trade up and down the Seine. The bridge
is a meeting place for groups of students, for lovers.

In summer the city is crowded with tourists. Sometimes
even the Parisians relax, those few who remain, as if to confirm that semi-miracles are possible. The latest dresses are
tried on. The girls bare their shoulders and the boys get
new tattoos. At times it seems a festival has come to town,
so light is the mood of the collective desire to slow down.
At other times the whole city is jittery with the teeth-
grinding excesses of too many strong espressos and the
attempt by the crush of visitors to diligently 'do' all the
tourist sights in world-record time. I maintain my own pace.

By July it is staying light until ten in the evening and
beyond. Long slow evenings when, in the course of my
walks, I realise the city is so soft that it has never fully settled into the contours of its design, even after so many
hundreds of years. The buildings as they stand are but the
preliminary sketches, and only with the falling of light do

they take shape. Paris is a city that has never accepted the hard-edged symmetry of its architecture, since it is forever busy fuzzing those edges with the graze of its grace.

On the Pont des Arts gnats hover, silhouetted against the pink sunset, around the trees in their neat boxes. The *bateaux-mouches*, the tourist boats, start to fill up. Their blinding arc lights shine up through the cracks of the bridge's wooden slats. Around 10 p.m. the pink drops out of the sky and the vapour trails from the jets flying southwards from Charles de Gaulle airport become purple against the weak blue.

I turn and cross to the opposite railing and stand looking in the other direction, east. The sky to the east, away from the setting sun, has darkened first. The river here is split in two by the Ile de la Cité. For a long time I stare at the split in the river, at its sharp stone point where two lovers sit beneath a single tree. The night hardens, the softness of the city secreting itself into the cracks between buildings, to rest and reappear at the next dusk. A split in the river. I think of what it means. You could go in two directions. Towards Matt. Towards the future. On the other side of the arrowhead-shaped Ile, the river meets itself again.

The true night begins at last. The indigo drops downwards and blankets the city, stone by stone, from the roofs down to the streets. The city darkens shade by shade, in much the same way I imagine that snow falling in still weather accretes itself onto buildings in greater and greater whitenesses.

But high in the sky, where the long-vanished sun, from around sunset's curve, still sends its rays to shine onto the upper atmosphere, there remain traces of light. I tilt my head upwards; light streams overhead, like the confluence of endless river systems: the rivers of photons that evening becomes. The streams tangle themselves together into vast silt estuaries, the muddied expanses between darkness and light, spilling ultimately into the deep ocean of night that expands on its own king tide to wash the blue atmosphere into nothingness.

Suddenly a flock of swallows reels chaotically, deeper and deeper into the dimness of the receding dusk. In their darting motions they seem to me a school of fish. At isolated moments—here is one, a school of birds in a tender Paris dusk—the pain of Matt's absence moves away by just a fraction, as if a cog has loosened on the wheel of grief. My eyes fill with tears once again. These are somehow good tears. The birds disappear, away to the depths of the river of night.

❧ *Tom*

I'VE LED A GOOD LIFE I'VE LED A GOOD LIFE I'VE LED A good life. Inside my father's head the many noises compete and from the chaos of machinery come headaches, blinding, monstrous, mindless. There are times, I imagine, when a single voice rises. This can either be a great relief—as when the giant propellors of a jet wind down and you notice finally the thin whine of a lone cicada—or its opposite: the high tension of concentrated malice as your ears ring in the silence. His weird fragmented diary continues.

After Matt dies, after those months alone, the television and hydroponics, the various Baxters and my leaving for the far side of the planet, I am awash in my own grief.

And in the meantime my father is furthering his disintegration. I will try my best to tell the story of the inside of his mind. I don't know how much of it I've got right. It only seems that this version of the story makes sense to me. Nobody could reach inside him now, not really. It is extraordinary how a human being can dry up, freeze, shut down. It is simply terrible, the frailty of the human mind.

'I've led a good life'—it's the voice of malice inside Tom's head, drowning out all the other voices. He clenches his jaw. He hears also—a sound from the real world—the grinding of his teeth.

He has stopped working. He sees a psychiatrist. It's a delayed reaction from the four years in prison, he's told. What you're undergoing could possibly be described as a very minor psychotic episode. But very minor. It's not all that uncommon. The doctor prescribes Melleril. Tom says he feels tired all the time. All this information is relayed to me, after his death, by Tess.

On Melleril all the voices and the machinery are still there. The only difference is that they seem to be coming from underwater. It's a hideous form of distortion in what he recognises as an already distorted situation.

And he knows now—and here is the truly tragic thing—he *knows* that he is losing his mind. He wants there to be something he can do about it. He knows it's all connected: Dan and Tess, prison, our drifting apart. I imagine that the love he feels for me is so powerful, his heart is scalded with the overload of pain. He can't stand the thought of losing me, but the truth begins to dawn on him: that he will die long before I do.

Losing his mind. It's a frightening image. To lose something like a mind, just like that. He can only picture simple things, like 'losing his wallet.' The sudden realisation, the panicked search through pockets, the double-checking, the trying to calm down and think, the going back over the day's events. When did I last see it? Was it at the supermarket? Did I have it out then? He is slipping down an icy slope. He will never find that moment to feel the warmth of the sun on the back of his neck. He is afraid. He wishes it were an all-consuming thing, but there remains a tiny corner where he sits and observes the descending turmoil. What he hates is that the corner is so small. He was a doctor, once; he could join the dots and make the leaps. There was a decent life. And now the world is shrinking to a point.

He reads nothing but chaos theory, unsure of whether it's good for him or not. He is interested in fractal geometry. It is a slender point of communication between us. First I feign interest and then it really grows. I will even take, at his urging, a couple of his chaos books to Paris. I will read them in a city whose very beauty is a chaos of beauty. After he is dead I will go through them again, try to make sense of the underlinings. He underlined the word 'fractal.' Fractal, I read, means any geometrical structure that has details on all scales of magnification. No matter how big or small you make it, you still see extra new details you didn't see before. Theoretically, then, infinite smallness is a fact: that is, a regression of scale that never ends.

Contradicting this, there is the infamous Planck Length. The physicist Max Planck suggested that the smallest physical structures—the smallest details—in the universe do actually have a minimum size-limit. We can go inwards and inwards and smaller and smaller for quite a while, but somewhere there in the exquisite distance is a rock bottom beyond which matter does not get any smaller. My father considers this to be a place of sleep and meditation where the consciousness of all things at last becomes inert, at peace. He remembers morphine: oh do not go gentle into that goodbye. It is suggested that the Planck Length is a million-million-million-million-millionth of a centimetre. (Approximately.) Beyond this, nothing.

But to my father, whose life is shrinking so rapidly, both options, infinite fractal regression or Planck's end-of-the-line, must be equally horrific.

It had begun years earlier, innocently enough, in a time devoid of innocence. In prison he had read Dr Mandelbrot's *The Fractal Geometry of Nature*. It was hard going, but he learnt some things. He knows from fractal geometry that the coastline of Britain is infinite. He knows that should he bend a thread, carefully, through every small twist and bend made by the outline of a map of Great Britain, he could then calculate the length of the coastline by measuring out the length of string against the map scale. He knows that should he do the same thing with a more detailed nautical map of the country, the coastline would be longer again. He knows that if he were to take a one-metre ruler and walk the entire coastline, measuring every nook and cranny, then the circumference of Great Britain would be very much larger than that which he had initially measured in the map. He knows that were he to measure it with, say, a one-centimetre rule, the length of the coastline of Britain would be vastly larger again.

And if you could measure the molecules along the water's edge with a ruler one photon in length? He realises, as Mandelbrot realised, that finally the idea of coastline disappears altogether, because one doesn't know any longer where is land and where is water.

In the same way that coastlines dissolve, so too, I imagine, does the idea of his life, and he feels already that he no longer knows what is his body and what is the memory that he will become.

He hopes that other books will help him. He goes back to some of his favourites. He tries to read some geometry, some physics, a biography of Franz Josef Liszt. His hands tremble and the words jump around on the page until the very page itself is nothing but a clean white surface on which a thousand black maggots writhe. I shiver to think of him dying so slowly like this.

There seems to be absolutely nothing for it but to weather it out. The Melleril does nothing but turn down the volume a little and muffle the high treble range. His mind is lost in a blizzard.

Before I leave for Paris, whenever he sees me, I sense the enormous effort he is making to hold back the tears. Later I always imagine his body trembling with the exhaustion of it. Perhaps I do nothing more for him now than define the huge gaps, the absences, the passage of time that has run riot through his own life. First you are this and then you are that. Time clunks forward and you mark best the changes by external events: falling leaves tell you of autumn, your daughter grown up is the heart-stab of loss. Around this time I am so far removed from the Isabelle he once had in his life. Who am I now? A young woman with her own concerns. I wonder if I could have changed anything, could have reached him. Where has he been? He thinks of prison and as always his heart starts to beat too rapidly. And the years since prison: where, indeed, has he been? Once upon a time he inhabited the earth.

He tries to remember me from the time before he was arrested. He writes about me in his diary. If he goes back far enough he can remember the joys of those earlier years, when I was a tiny flame-haired fairy prancing through our world, and we lived in a tight triangle of Tom and Tess and me. Rectangle if you include Uncle Dan. But when he tries to move to my early adolescence, the clarity of his memory begins to fade, as if at this point the two of us, father and daughter, had begun to recede from each other's lives. Was it she or I who went away? he thinks. And then he is inundated by a wave of guilt. Of course, he thinks.

It was me, Tom. Tess had proved love to be a betrayal. And yet I can't stop loving her, he thinks: she is all I have, for half a life. But Isabelle is my one and only. My best and closest, my fountain of joy. And what did I do around this time, when Isabelle was a teenager?

I started staying at work forever. I started cramming in the patients. I started falsifying Medicare records. I started the long haul that would lead six years later to imprisonment. The whole thing developed a momentum that after a while seemed pointless to arrest. It was money, of course. It was greed. I can't deny that. I thought that if I had unlimited money then I could prove to Tess that I was the best. Ever since Dan, whenever that happened, it was like she had gone away from me. Was unable to come back.

Fuck my brother. Fuck you, Dan. I loved Tess. How could I stand in her way? These were human things: desire, or lust, I don't know how to give them names, I don't know what they really mean. No longer know. I thought that, with enough money, it was you that I would hurt, not Tess, not Isabelle. And yet family works this way: I go to my grave without confronting you, because that's how families work. That's how family works. And I wish it was otherwise, so fuck you. You fucked my wife—for how long, I don't even want to know—so fuck you.

All that was in his diary, too. A difficult book to read, even today. He can't hold on to a train of thought for too long. Anger and guilt and self-condemnation attack him incessantly like obscene filthy birds. Isabelle, Isabelle. Where was I? he thinks. He was trying to think about Isabelle. But now his mind has jumped to Tess.

It is summer in 1965. They are buying an ice-cream at Balmoral Beach. Tom is wearing a towelling hat. A thick triangle of Pinke Zinke cream protects his nose. Tess is nineteen years old. To Tom it seems she radiates light.

Tess is wearing tight blue and white checked pants. They are low-slung at the hips and come up short above the ankles. Sandals, and a cotton shirt tied above the belly button. And Tom is thinking, I don't know much, but I know I can grow old with this girl.

'Let's get our stuff,' he says.

They run to the car, a '48 Packard, and pull out towels and bathing costumes. When they emerge from the change rooms in the pavilion they hold hands as they walk onto the sand. There are children everywhere, and the screech of birds, and the soft lap of the harbour water, the absence of waves which settles in the air like hypnosis.

They spread out their towels and lie down and doze for a while. When it becomes too hot they go into the water, breast-stroking out towards the shark barrier. They pause and gain their breath, smiling at each other. Tom holds on with one arm to the support pillar and with the other pulls Tess close to him. Their legs entangle underwater. The sunlight makes speckles in Tess's eyes, and drops of water hang suspended and glinting on her long lashes. As they kiss,

Tom cannot exactly work out which thing is more delicious: the coolness inside her mouth or the taste of salt that settles on his tongue.

That night at dinner, at a restaurant in Chinatown, Tom proposes to Tess; so the day, and the beach, are always to have a special significance, and as I grow up I'm told the story many times. A few years later, when Tess is pregnant with me, and so near full-term that her eating habits have become truly bizarre, Tom wakes before dawn one morning and finds her in the kitchen, ravenously polishing off ice-cream and trying to butter Sao biscuits at the same time.

'Let's go to the beach,' she grins, the vanilla ice-cream dripping from the sides of her mouth. 'I really feel like a swim!'

They arrive at Balmoral just after 6 a.m. on a deserted weekday morning. Tess's bulbous, shining stomach fits into no known bathing costume, or at least none she's willing to buy.

'I'll swim in my underpants and bra!' she exclaims.

Tom, always more circumspect, frowns and says, 'Are you sure that'll be all right here?'

Tess laughs and pats her stomach. 'What are they going to do, arrest a pregnant woman?' She kisses him on the cheek. 'Anyway, I've got you here to fight them off.'

They walk down to the water across the crisp morning sand. Tom stands admiring the view; the harbour surface is pulled tight like a mirror. He watches Tess disrobing.

'Aren't you going to come in?' she says.

'No, it's too cold. You're the one who's crazy!'

She stands still for a moment, her underpants almost disappearing beneath the bulge of her belly, her inflated breasts resting expectantly on the beginning of that grand curve.

Tom thinks that small flames might flare out from his fingertips, such a burning love does he feel for Tess and for the baby she carries inside her, and for their future. Our future.

Tess moves into the still water, spreading out the first ripples of the morning, her arms trailing behind her and her fingertips gliding on the surface as she descends gradually to her waist. Tom sits down on the sand and hugs his knees to his chin. 'I love you so much,' I'm sure he murmurs into his pullover.

'Owww, Tom! Ohh, God, it's so-o-o cold!' Tess turns and faces him, her face split from ear to ear by the brightest smile he's ever seen. She jumps up and down on the spot. Tom watches her stomach, in which lies curled their baby, me, as it bobs above the water and submerges, bobs and submerges.

'I can't go under,' she cries, breathless.

'You can do it,' he urges. 'You can do it, Tess.'

She takes a deep breath, holds her nose and drops into the enveloping water. For an instant Tom watches the ripples scramble in a miniature mayhem where she disappears; then, almost immediately, the water bulges upwards and her slicked golden head breaks the surface as she shoots up into the air, squealing, 'I did it! I did it!'

A month later I am born.

I have tried to explain that my father was not well for many years. He so slowly went away that I could turn my attention to other things. He was going away in prison, he was going away through my years with Matt, he was already a great distance away when Matt died. He was closer than ever to gone as I headed off to Europe. I don't know that I've got the details right. I've tried to create the whole thing, but it's all, as I've said, such a fog. All just a guess at what was inside someone else. And it was extraordinary, the relief I felt at boarding that airplane for Paris.

I've led a good life I've led a good life I've led a good life. My father's head continues to pound, through the Melleril, through his deepest sleep, through his dreams. He dreams repeatedly of Danny Boyle, who died in prison, his head caved in by a frenzied attack with two billiard balls tied inside a woollen sock. Danny Boyle the informer, the dog. Prison treachery, nothing to do with Tom; he didn't even want to know. Tom had hardly even spoken to Danny—they had nothing to say—but he had been fascinated, from a distance, by the young ratbag's cocky sarcasm. On the morning shift in the kitchen roster, it was Tom who had found Danny in the pantry, the floor dark red like a skating rink of blood, Danny's head so flattened and distorted that at first Tom had thought it was a joke, some mannequin, perhaps, placed by the prison officials to test Tom's reactions.

In the dreams Danny is always alive, swaying in the corridor, his head pulped and his shoulders smeared with flecks of brain, smiling at Tom through the blood. 'I'll be all right,' he's saying. 'I'll be all right. Just give me a minute to catch my breath.' And when Tom tries to touch him, to reach out his arm and steady him, it is always the same. Danny waves him away with a nonchalant flick of his hand. 'No, no, I'm fine. A minute is all I need. A minute to catch my breath.'

But the image of Danny Boyle, alive yet dead, is so frightening that often Tom wakes up at this moment. It is the deep heart of night, the hour before dawn. The absence of sound is made the more evident by his panicked breathing and the thud of his heart. The words are always lingering from the dream as he sits upright in the bed and stares into the darkness. A minute to catch my breath.

Zooming

SUMMER SOFTENS INTO EARLY AUTUMN. MY FRENCH continues to improve. I get two shifts a week working at the bar of a tiny smoky nightclub near Pigalle. I want to make my money last. I meet the captain and we get drunk at a brasserie one golden afternoon in which it seems even the swallows are bursting with excess energy. The crowds move along the Boulevard St Germain in a pleasant blur. Our meeting begins with a coincidence and ends in a three-day affair. Affair is a strange word. I like the French equivalent: *aventure*. Adventure. Sitting at my sidewalk table, I notice the beautiful woman at the table beside me: tall and pale with black hair and black eyes; high cheekbones and a thin face and luscious lips, in her early forties perhaps. The woman looks up. We smile at each other. I am reading Matthiesson's *The Snow Leopard* and I look at her book and see that it is Lampedusa's *The Leopard,* in English. It's reason enough to talk.

'That's a beautiful book,' I say. I hold mine up. 'We're almost reading the same thing.'

The woman studies my cover. 'I haven't read that one,' she says. 'Is it good?'

'It's great.'

'So…I suppose you could say what separates us is the snow.'

'Right, the snow.'

'Where are you from?'

We move to the same table and don't stop talking for hours. The woman is Laura Almeida, briefly a Portuguese screen star in her early twenties who was too strong—it's her own strange description—even for cinema. Preferring a life at sea and a man in every port, she joined the Portuguese merchant navy at twenty-three. Eventually she became a captain in charge of the largest cargo ships, at thirty-five. Now she's forty-three and lives in Lisbon, and is in Paris—'We're nowhere near the ocean,' she laughs, 'but it's a good junket'—for an international conference of ships' captains. She speaks five languages, including flawless English and French.

And I know immediately that she is anchored in the centre of her heart. As this woman, this force, moves through my life for three days, I feel a rush of vertigo, a luminous pull.

We talk all afternoon, switch from coffee to wine. It seems we've been friends for a lifetime, so comfortable do we feel with each other. A little drunk, we go back to Laura's hotel. That night, for the first time since high school, I kiss a woman. Her conference is over and the weekend stretches ahead. I experience for the first time the full impact of desire for someone of my own sex. Laura Almeida is a sinewy goddess naked on the bed. For three days we make love and when we are not making love we talk and order room service and watch cable TV or walk the streets of Paris. It is a tender time. On the second day I go home to get some rest and a change of clothes. I ring Laura, who answers drowsily in the hotel room.

'My body feels filled and empty at the same time,' I say. 'I was catching the metro home. Even when I cross my legs I'm tingling.' Later that night I return and fall into her arms once more.

'We may never see each other again,' Laura says. 'I hope we do, but it happens: you meet people, you never see them again. Come to Lisbon some time, by all means. But I'll be with my husband and kids.'

'So here we are then.' I laugh. 'Trapped in the middle of the beautiful today.'

We tell each other stories. There is little room for sleep. There are ten million people in Paris yet dawn comes to the city like a cool private whisper of light swishing through the roses in the flowerbox that hangs outside the French windows.

'There's usually not much point talking about sex,' I say, 'but I have to tell you this. When I came before it was…it was…it's hard to describe.'

'But try. I want to know.'

'Okay. Let me see. You know those kitsch kind of lamp things from the sixties—it's a globe of glass, and when you touch it, the forks of light scatter out to reach your fingers, kind of like lightning?'

'I know those things.'

'Yeah. A little container of lightning. That's the image I'm thinking of. There's one of those down there, between my legs. The light was flickering and sparking and beginning to grow more intense. And then all the tiny forks of lightning gathered together and—phoom!—turned into this single ray of light. Maybe it shot off through my head.'

'And it's out there wandering the streets.'

'Yeah, a UFO. A sexual UFO! Completely crazy, zapping all the tourists on the Boulevard St Michel!'

Later she says, 'This is more than coincidence. The way it happened—bang. Do you believe in coincidence?'

'I believe different things on different days,' I say. 'Maybe it's just that coincidence is such a beautiful thing.'

'Maybe. Well, whatever. But I feel something good with you. Do you know what synchronicity is? The fortuitous intermeshing of events. An old sailor in New Orleans told me that once. His name was Zuzu. He spoke perfect English. He was always drunk, but that's exactly what he said. How could I forget words like that? Especially when

I had to look them up in my dictionary that night. Synchronicity: the fortuitous intermeshing of events. But how do you think those events come about? There was a scientist once who was talking about the way progress is made. He said, "Yes, but did you ever observe to *whom* the good accidents happen? Chance favours only the prepared mind." You have to be open to the arrival of these things. And here we are, arrrriving at each other.'

We lie silent for a long time. It must be 6 a.m. The doors to the balcony are wide open and the wind chimes Laura has hung—'my travelling music'—tinkle gently. The dawn birds of Paris are beginning to pipe and twitter and from somewhere in the distance the cooing of pigeons drifts to us from the lintels of the old university buildings.

We tell each other everything: on and off for three days our lives unravel, backwards, like skeins of coloured threads trailing behind us.

'I may be thin but I'm very strong when I need to be,' says Laura. 'I'm good at physical things—swimming, drawing, steering a boat. When I started in the merchant marine, they had me doing all the shitty jobs that everyone has to do—testing me, because they thought I was so frail, to see if I could do the same jobs as the men. And of course I could. They had me hanging by ropes down a forty-foot hold, scrubbing the walls, suspended there. I loved it. I did it all. I had the brains, I had the guts, I had the willingness, and of course I had the physical strength.'

Watching her talk, I am distracted. I lean over, kiss her softly.

'Tell me another story,' I say, a while later.

'It's funny you say that,' says Laura. 'I've already been wondering whether I should do that. I'm going to tell you something I don't tell often, to anyone. Just because most people would think me crazier than I already am. A little too crazy, this story. But true: you see, that's the beauty of it. I'll tell you this story because it's about strong bonds. It's about sensing things. It's about recognising when someone important passes through your life.

'This has happened with you, you see. My meeting with you. Our coming together like this. And I'm going to tell you about something that happened seventeen years ago, something that happened to me out of the blue— just like that—in New Orleans again. Like in that cafe three days ago.

'But before you think I'm crazy, let me explain one thing. I'm Portuguese, okay? And we are not like other Europeans. I think what makes Portugal a nation is the sea all around it. Or not exactly all around it. But it's an island, surrounded by Spain to the north and east and by the Atlantic to the west and south. I think that between the known evil of Spain and the unknown ocean—which could bring hope, you see—the Portuguese people always chose the ocean, regardless of politics or religion or trade.

'It means that Portugal is a port, and above all a port of departure. There's the eternal desire to leave, to go some other place, to be somebody else, and not to think of Portugal as a nation in itself. This creates an eternal dissatisfaction. It's what we're known for. Portuguese have the sailor's sense of never being at home. That's why *I'm* a sailor. We've discovered a new emotion for ourselves and we call it *saudade*—'

'Say it again.'

'*Saudade*.'

'*Saudade*. It's beautiful. What is it?'

'It's a dwelling on our sadness, a longing for another time. A nostalgia, even for things you've never experienced. We sing of it in the music we call *fado*—that means fate. I don't know if *saudade* was born with the sea or if the sea was born with *saudade*. It doesn't matter. *Saudade* starts with the sea, and *fado* too. The simple fact of going to sea, leaving family and lovers behind, meant *saudade* for everyone. But it's much better to be a sailor than an actress, you know. An actress just gets surrounded by bad people— everyone wants a piece of you; they don't have enough of their own. But a sailor learns to become herself.

'Where was I? Ah—the story! Yes. I have no idea where I was going with that. So. Seventeen years ago. I was—let me see—I was twenty-six years old. I was working on the freighter *Peter Pan* out of Lisbon. We were in New Orleans. I had a date with a boy I'd met—dinner and a movie. A sweet guy. I had a great time in those years. I was wild. I made love with a lot of people. They couldn't keep up with me. Then I'd go to sea, and I loved my solitude and the hard work. Anyway, we were in this cafe in New Orleans. When the waiter walked up to us I looked at him and I felt I'd been hit. I was dizzy. I *knew* this man—you know what I mean? I mean, I *knew* him. I knew him from somewhere. The closeness I felt to this person was intense.

'I had to play it down a bit—I mean, I was on a date with this other fellow. Besides, it was pretty obvious that this waiter was gay. That wasn't the point. I was obsessed with him—couldn't get him out of my mind. I went back to the cafe the next day and thank God he was there. We talked a little and organised to meet the next Friday for a coffee. I was open with him; what else could I be? I said, "I feel something strong here. That's why I came back." He said, "So do I. It's weird." It had been obvious that he felt something about me, too. So the Friday. That would be my last full day in New Orleans.'

'What was his name?'

'Daniel. His name was Daniel McLaren. So there's three days before we meet, and I'm so obsessed, he's in my mind so much, that it's really getting to me. How do you say it in English? It was bugging me. What's going on here? I asked myself. I was getting nervous. It almost felt like a supernatural thing. I was a realist back then, you know. If I could touch it, then I believed in it. For one whole day I lie on my bunk in my cabin and try to calm down. Outside the boat, the port is busy—have you ever been to New Orleans?'

'No.'

'It's a great place. Wild, a little kooky. Do you know this word?'

'Yeah, kooky. Yeah, okay.'

'So I'm trying to calm down. I'm…*meditating*. Maybe that's what I'm doing. I mean, I've actually become worried about why I'm so excited about meeting this guy, about what the hell is going on. So I'm saying, "Think, Laura, think. What is it about him? Do you know him from somewhere?" Or maybe I'm praying—I didn't believe in God, of course: "God, help me out here. Explain to me what's going on."

'A whole day on my bunk. I remember the reflection of water coming through the porthole in the middle of the day. It was like this liquid pattern shimmering on the ceiling.

'Now here's where it gets weird. I'm telling you this, but I don't tell many people. I'm awake, but I go into some kind of trance—I really do. I'm no longer in the cabin, I'm no longer on the ship. All of a sudden I'm in a cottage. It's all pretty primitive—a fire, a big pot, a dirt floor. I'm aware of everything, the smells, the texture of my dress. It's all unfamiliar but it's totally real. I can see the dirt beneath my fingernails. And I know it's Ireland. I know it's a couple of hundred years ago.'

Oh dear, I think. 'Wow,' I say. But it's a lame wow. There had to be a catch, I think. Past lives. I should be going soon.

But Laura continues. 'It's not a pleasant place. A man is screaming at a woman. It's my mother and father. He starts to hit her. Is this Daniel? I say to myself. No, it's not him. But I seem to have the power to move around in this dream, or whatever it is. So then suddenly I'm a little older. It's still Ireland, the same area, but a different cottage. And I know what I've done. I've married someone, to escape that situation, the parents, the madness, the fighting. But I'm terribly unhappy. It's turned out that my husband is drunk all the time. I'm terrified. He's walking up the path and I can hear the crunch of his feet on the gravel and he's about to come in the door and I know at some point soon he will find a reason to hit me, hard. I'm in my cabin on board the *Peter Pan* in New Orleans but I'm also in this cottage in Ireland and it's not pleasant but I know I have to solve this mystery. Is this awful man Daniel? I ask myself. And I know the answer: no, this is not him either.

'I'm out of the cottage before he starts beating me. What I mean is, I go to a different part of the dream. And now I'm so sad, it's almost unbearable. I've never felt this sad in all my life—I mean me, Laura, not whoever I am in the dream. It's like I'm two people. I'm walking across these fields towards these dark cliffs. There's nobody around. As I come closer I can hear the noise of the waves on the rocks getting louder and louder. Some other things become apparent to me. My name is Kathleen. My hair is being blown about me by the wind. Then I'm at the edge of the cliff. I feel this sadness like a tiredness that goes down to my toes.

'Now it's really terrifying, being in this trance but half-aware, not able to leave it, knowing there's something to be solved, a question I want answered. And then I realise I'm here to commit suicide. And I'm looking down at the rocks and suddenly my despair is so great that I am no longer scared. I am resigned to the fact that I'm about to jump down to the rocks so far below. They're jagged and black.

'And then I'm aware of this…this…*presence* beside me. It's like a glowing of white light. Okay. It's a person there. It's a new person in my trance, in my dream. I try to turn to see what he looks like, but I can't really turn and he remains like a shimmer. And then I'm filled with this beautiful light, which is obviously a part of the light beside me, and in an instant my sadness becomes a joy that even today is impossible to describe. My name is Kathleen, I'm twenty-two years old, and I've led a miserable life. Here I am on this bleak cliff and I am about to die, to escape from everything. And this presence is beside me, and then it's inside me, and I feel a love I've never felt before. Oh God, it's so pure, this feeling.'

'Is it Daniel?'

'Yes, yes, yes. It's Daniel. At this point I ask myself the question, and the answer is obvious—I know it sounds crazy, but this is the boy in the cafe in New Orleans, without any doubt. But why can't I see him? It doesn't make sense. It's not like he's real, like my husband or my father— I mean Kathleen's husband or father. I can't see him. It's really just the feeling of him that's there.

'So I don't jump off the cliff. I walk back to my life, across the fields, down the hills, to my village. I know I'm in Donegal, on the north-west coast of Ireland. I don't know how much my life has changed but I know that I feel different. I know from the glow that I'm all right now, that I'll survive. Somehow I'm protected and safe, even if things are bad.

'Now Laura wants to know more. Who is Daniel? Where did he come from? What was he doing on that cliff? So I try to move around in the trance again. It seems so easy. I just tell myself, go where it is necessary to find more information. And I'm there. Do you think this is stupid?'

'No, no,' I half-lie. 'Go on. I want to hear more.'

'It's a bit further in the future now. Not too far. A year maybe. It hasn't been good, living with my mad husband. But every time there's violence, I can draw on my memory of that white light on the cliff. And be safe. It's a cold cloudy day and I'm way up in the back field digging potatoes. I just can't tell you how vivid this all is. I'm on the bunk in New Orleans but I can *smell* those potatoes and that soil, you know? I can feel the weight of that potato in my hand and I can see my hand drop it into the sack that's tied around my waist. And from far across the fields, from the other side of the small harbour, I can hear the church bells begin to peal. It's the way sound comes to you on the wind, from far away. You can barely hear it, but it's there.

'I stand up straight and listen to the bells. It's not Sunday. There's only one explanation. Fishermen have drowned. The bodies have been found. And I know that my husband is dead. And I'm happy—really happy, for the first time since the light by the cliff. No, I'm more than happy. I feel all my heaviness float away from my body, up into the clouds. I know I'm going to go through the motions of the mourning widow, but the truth is, I'm joyful. My husband is dead. I'm twenty-three years old. Life can begin.

'There was one more move in the trance. It's a couple of years further on. It's the day of my wedding. My second wedding. I can feel the excitement. There's a lot of activity in the house of my beloved. Little girls everywhere, soon to be my nieces. My husband-to-be is a fisherman, too, a captain, a handsome man, older but calm, a man with a generous spirit. I know all this just from being in the trance. The trance tells me we'll have children and we'll live together until old age and not be unhappy.

'For a moment I'm alone in the room where I'm preparing myself for the wedding. And in that moment, suddenly, there is Daniel beside me again. The shimmering light spreads out from where he stands. It fills the room. It is a moment of closeness, intense beyond imagining. I'm so happy. But I'm sad, too. He is going away now, and I know we will never meet again, that the white light will go forever and leave nothing but the traces of its warmth.'

Laura rolls over onto her side on the huge hotel bed, to get more comfortable.

'Phew, long story. Are you still with me?'

'I'm with you,' I say, my head resting on the crook of my elbow, staring at Laura's lips and eyes as the story spills out.

'At last, I come out of the trance. Out of the state. We're back in New Orleans now, okay? I look at the clock on the cabin wall. Two hours have passed. I'm exhausted. My body is tingling and light. I've just had a supernatural experience, the first one in my life. I'm twenty-six years old and I laugh: I figure if I was that way inclined, I would have known about it by now! And the dream, or whatever it was, has told me a lot of things. But it didn't tell me one big thing: who the fuck was Daniel? All I know is that the boy in the cafe who I'm seeing on Friday and the glowing light in the dream are the same person.

'It makes no sense. I think it's meaningless, I think it's crazy, I kind of ignore it. I try to ignore it. But it's so strong. I have a logical mind. I'm proud of that, right? I've never even thought about this weird kind of nonsense. I tell myself, okay. Laura. This is nothing. This is perfectly all right. Perfectly normal. This is what your imagination has invented, to come up with an explanation for your reaction to Daniel, for your feelings about him. It's a bizarre explanation, but that's your imagination and you can be proud of it.

'And I say to myself, no matter what, do *not* tell him about this on Friday. It's just too bizarre. If you tell him this story he will listen politely and then he'll excuse himself and go to the bathroom and find a window to climb through and get out of there as fast as possible without even paying for his drink. He will never even say goodbye.

'So Friday comes. We meet in a bar at the pre-arranged time. I was pretty good with men, always knew what I was doing. But I was nervous in this situation. It was the power of it, you know. I didn't feel in control. And a gay man, too. And it wasn't directly sexual—though we did end up making love twice, a couple of years later, but that's another story.

'We meet. We order drinks. And then, guess what? Maybe it's to break the tension—I blurt the story out. I can't believe I'm doing it, but once I've started I don't seem to be able to stop. The crazy story is pouring out and inside my head I'm saying to myself, here's the end of a beautiful friendship, before it even starts. I tell him everything I've just told you. Only probably in a lot more detail, because this is seventeen years ago, and maybe my memory has faded a bit. At the end I blow out a big breath. I feel kind of naked.

'He just sits there silent, staring down at his drink. He's got these lines running across his forehead, like a frown, like he's concentrating. They're the longest seconds of my life. And then he sighs. He looks up at me and shakes his head. He seems to have gone very quiet. He almost looks upset. "I always knew that one day I'd meet Kathleen," he says. And he tells me this incredible story. You ready for more?'

'Keep going. I'm listening.'

'Okay. He grew up in Akron, Ohio. You know where that is? It's a pretty straight place, somewhere in the middle. It's football and cheerleaders, that kind of place. By the

time he was twelve or thirteen he was an outsider at his
high school. He told me he already knew he was gay by
then, and that was fine, but the problem was that the rest
of the world knew too. He hated every minute of it. He
had six brothers and sisters, in a busy, close family, very
stars and stripes. The family was kind enough but there
was no gentleness, no privacy, no solitude in his life. He
dreaded going to school. He was always being teased and
pushed about. He'd rush home from school at the end of
each day. If he was quick, there was a time in the afternoon, for an hour or less, when he might have some time
to himself. He would go into his room, which he shared
with some older brothers, and lie down on his bed and try
to relax. In this way he discovered, on his own, how to
survive the awful times at school.

'So every afternoon he'd lie on his bed. Doing absolutely
nothing. Just staring at the ceiling. And after a while of
doing this every day, he felt something start to happen. He
floated up above himself. He could look back over his
shoulder and see the room from a different perspective. He
said the first time he saw himself down there, lying on the
bed with his eyes shut, he got a shock. But it's comfortable and he keeps doing it. He had this special thing. He
discovered this special, secret thing. After a while he can
leave the room and travel around the neighbourhood. It
was just like flying, he said, without making any effort.
Every afternoon he left his body behind in the bedroom
and the ghost part of him zoomed around Akron.

'Eventually he's doing this thing with perfect ease. Like getting better at driving, yeah? And he starts shooting off into space. It's just a progression, you see. Once you've made the first step, the move away from the body, the question of distance becomes less important. He said there was nothing profound about this. He wasn't really aware of what he was doing; it was just for thrills, like a roller coaster. He was a thirteen-year-old boy. He loves the way he can go straight up, on and on. He said the sky turned from blue to black really fast. He said when there was no more atmosphere there was no more sound, just the silences of space.

'But the thing he loved the most was building up speed on the return from space. There's the curve of the earth coming into view now and there's the United States and there's the Great Lakes and suddenly he's swooped down into daylight and Akron takes shape and he can let himself glide down to his street and his house.

'Then one day something happens. He plunges back to earth from space and he bursts into the light of atmosphere and—bang! He doesn't know where he is. It's not Ohio! He's hovering in the air above a high cliff and a wild sea. It's very green countryside and it's almost deserted. There's a woman with long hair in a long dress standing on the edge of the cliff, looking down at the water. And Daniel can feel the woman's despair, and suddenly the roller-coaster game is no longer just play. You've got to remember, this is a young boy. He's not sure what's going on. Can you imagine?'

'I'm trying to imagine,' I say. 'I'm trying to get past my goose bumps.'

'Well, yes, you know what's coming, don't you? He said he just went down lower out of curiosity at first. She was the only person for miles around. When he came closer, he knew she was about to jump. And he wanted to save her, to stop her. He thought if the two of them together could share their loneliness, then they would no longer be lonely and she would not need to die. All he did was try to move closer to her. He told me he only wanted to do two things: to stroke her hair and to tell her it was all right. That's all he did, he said. He was stroking her hair but his hand moved right through it. He tried to give her all his love. "What's your name?" he said to her. "Kathleen," she said. He stood behind her stroking her hair for as long as it took to know that she would live now. He stood for a long time, so happy to be in love. Then he opened his eyes in the bedroom in Akron.

'He tried to go there again but it never worked. For a year or more he continued to leave his body at will, but he couldn't find Kathleen or the place where he'd first seen her. And then suddenly one afternoon, without even trying, he was there. But not at the cliffs. He was about two miles away, in a village on a harbour by the sea where Kathleen was to be married that day. And somehow he knew he was saying goodbye. He found her alone in a room. "I have to go now," he told me he said, "but everything gets better from here for you, and life will be good."

'Do you see what happened? Her life had meaning from the point where she met him, and his had meaning from saving her. Up until they met, both of them thought they had no use in the world. Of course, *everyone* has a particular use in the world. It's a matter of finding out what that is. There's a whole lot of people living without purpose. He never saw her again after that day. He told me he watched the wedding from a high distance, but that already Akron was growing stronger. We were sitting in that dingy bar in New Orleans and it seemed he'd been talking for a very long time. We'd barely touched our drinks. I just sat there, dumbfounded. I asked him, "What then?"

'"After that," he said. "After that, I somehow survived high school, I gradually forgot about my little ability— *zooming* is what I'd named it—and life rolled on. In Akron I taught myself, through pain, that it's okay to be different. Then I moved to New York—where else would you go?—and learnt that it's good to be gay. And here I am: in a bar with you in New Orleans. Total strangers and yet evidently not. I just can't believe this is happening. I mean, I *can,* but I'd sort of forgotten to expect it. I did always know that I'd one day meet Kathleen. I just didn't know that she'd be a Portuguese sailor called Laura!"'

I finally laugh, a release of air and tension. 'Wow,' I tell her, 'I don't know what to say.' We lie for a while stroking each other's faces. My head is swirling with her story. My body has floated away, as if the last three days have existed in a spirit-world. As I stroke her I try to consider what our meeting could mean. She may not be telling me what my use in the world is; I would never expect or presume as my due the luxury of such assistance. But surely she is pointing out that such a search is worthwhile, is possibly all there is. The Great Worthwhile. With a jolt the image enters my mind that on the prow of some ship, on a vast expanse of ocean, I inhale the wind, and into me flood the vagabond aromas, the sandalwood and spices, of that port, my home, where I have never been. Meeting Laura brings me closer to the horizon that I am watching unceasingly. Laura is a blink in my unflinching gaze and yet in that single blink I surrender, let go, relax and learn all there is to know, in a dream world, where time expands like a mushroom cloud. And whether the story of Kathleen and Daniel is true seems less important than the fact that two people, however bizarre the circumstances, have made a link. My heart is out of kilter with the world, and it is a form of salvation to assume this is only a temporary condition.

'So, Isabelle.' Laura snaps me out of my thoughts. 'Let's get room service. Some breakfast. I'm starving. And then *we'll* say goodbye, though maybe not forever.' She kisses me on the forehead. 'Hot chocolate and a tartine to dip in it, or some croissants.'

'That sounds good.'

'Like I said, I tell it rarely. Well, you can see why. It's a true story. Bonds and recognition. I'm not saying I ever dropped in on you from space when you were Cleopatra. I'm just saying there is no coincidence. I'm just saying that if the mind is prepared for the necessary thing to arrive in it, then sometimes, if providence is moving, that thing will appear. It's not miraculous, as in unexplained magic. But being at sea for long enough has taught me that life is a miracle. Even if for many people it stops short. And what a shame. You know, I believe you have to work pretty hard to close your mind to wonder. But most of the world succeeds.'

'So do you believe it?'

'Do I believe what exactly?'

'Well, you know, the whole thing.'

'I don't know what I believe. All I know for sure is that what happened on the bunk in my cabin was real. It may have only been a very strong dream, but it was a real dream. And it happened *after* I met Daniel in the cafe. And the story he told me was after my dream. Maybe he's just weird, insecure, a compulsive liar. Maybe after I told the dream to him, he made up that story on the spot. Anything is possible.'

We laugh. 'Well, it's a damned good story either way,' I say. 'Do you ever see him?'

'We stayed friends. We kept in touch for ten years or more. Then we had a falling out. It was one of those stupid things, some trivial reason. I always planned I would get back in touch, patch things up. It was just temporary. You get angry then a while later you swallow your pride. Real friendship is elastic like that, you see. But that was it. A couple of years later I found out he'd died.'

'How'd he die?'

'You know, AIDS. Pneumonia from AIDS. God, he was sweet.'

'Life is short.'

'That's right. That's what *fado* understands. That's what *saudade* understands. That everything is departure.'

Snow

MY BRIEF TIME WITH LAURA LOOPS IN MY MIND like some bizarre and joyful fragment of a super-8 film. It is hard to understand that if Matt had not died then I would not have come to Paris and would not have met her. The months bleed together until winter comes. In December in Paris I experience weather colder than I've ever known before. And snow, which I've waited a lifetime to see and to touch. It's the Australian condition. North of the Snowy Mountains, at least. For as long as I can remember I have tried to imagine the texture of snow. Christmas in Australia—the sizzling hot days, the sunburn, the flies—made snow a substance rarer than gold, more exotic than titanium.

The fortuitous intermeshing of events. And how the sublime emerges from pain. Like everything else that happens after the death of Matt, there is a hallucinatory quality to my experience with snow. At times I come to believe that something has changed in the way my eyes work.

I remember once reading about an argument creationists employed to try to debunk the theory of evolution. How can an eye, they argued, develop in stages, *towards* being an eye, without functioning as an eye? But I know that the spirit can develop by just such bizarre leaps. It's called punctuated equilibrium. Nothing much happens for a long time, and then everything happens at once.

In November there are strikes and street protests all over France. I'm a little too busy coping with shop transactions and the day-to-day challenge of living to understand very clearly the subtleties of European trade economics and the mood of the French people. It's as if electrodes are attached all over my skin, infusing me with new sensations, and the strikes are only one of a thousand things to take in.

Then in December there's a general strike of all the transport workers in Paris. The metro, the RER, the buses all shut down. The universities cancel all classes and many businesses close for the duration. The city sighs at the uninvited break. Cars disappear from the streets. It's a miniholiday. The Parisians actually seem relaxed. The *mairie* of Paris makes available, free to the public, the tourist barges, the *bateaux-mouches*. It's not much in terms of getting around but I decide to make use of this odd form of transport.

It's a cold still evening and in a cafe I overhear a woman at the next table saying, 'It might snow tonight.' I go back to my apartment and luxuriate in the central heating. When I wake in the morning my eyes snap open and I am immediately, fully awake, without grogginess. I know that something is different but for a moment I'm not sure what it could be. I sniff hard and smell a sharp tang in the air.

'This is it!' I exclaim. 'This must be it!' I jump out of bed. My body is light as if I am filled with helium. But I look out the window and it is not snowing yet.

Still, it's a light I have never seen before. The sky is heavy with brilliant white clouds. When I look directly into the centre of the clouds their edges contain flecks of silver. So in Paris it is true about silver linings!

I climb into the shower. 'Please God, please God, let it snow today,' I say. Even though He quite possibly does not exist, He is my special friend whenever I am keen about things. The bathroom fills with steam.

The streets of the Latin Quarter are eerily empty. I am warm in my boots and overcoat but I can see that the asphalt is iron cold. It is eight o'clock in the morning. For two or three minutes I walk down the centre of Rue St Jacques and not a single car comes towards me. The brittle air is tinged with blueness: the colour of expectancy.

I stop in at Le Week-End Brasserie and take a table overlooking the street. The occasional car moves by but the usually hectic intersection is relatively still. I watch the rugged-up workers unloading the truck across the road at the fruit shop. Pallets of summer: clementines from Portugal, glowing bright orange like buns deep inside an oven; passionfruits from Kenya; mangoes from the Ivory Coast; huge Spanish strawberries.

I read my book for a while. When I look up, a white flake flutters to the ground in slow motion. For a moment I think it is a piece of fluff or feather-down from someone shaking a quilt out a window. Then more flakes are falling and I know it is snowing. Suddenly the intersection is draped in this soft downwardness of white.

I have encountered a new marvel. I sit absolutely still with my palms pressed flat on the table and a pot of tea in front of me. Steam rises from the spout. The wide expanse of concertina window acts as a frame on the street scene being swished into whiteness. I know that the moment will not last forever so the next best thing is to be calm and keep my eyes wide open. I sink into a reverie of acute awareness brought on by the lowering of heartbeat and pulse.

I study the snow. Soon, I know, I will walk outside to touch it, in case it doesn't last too long. But for the moment I simply watch it. I try to focus on individual snowdrops; then I try to take in the whole scene. It's a windless day. I realise that the snowflakes do not flutter like leaves or feathers. Rather, they seem to fall to earth with a gentle and resigned heaviness. And yet at the very next instant I think of them as near-weightless things brushed over some ledge in the sky and moving towards earth with only the faintest of responses to the laws of gravity.

A car moves along the street and for a moment the flakes horizontal with the line traced by its passing roof tumble and jiggle in the turbulence of its slipstream. An invisible cone of heat rises from the exhaust pipe of the fruit truck and the snowflakes jostle to move away from that too. But despite these minor fluctuations, the inter-section of Rue Gay Lussac and Rue St Jacques, seen from Le Week-End Brasserie, is an arena that contains this end-less repetition of white falling lazily upon itself.

My little horse must think it queer
To stop without a farmhouse near—

I try to remember the words to Frost's poem, but it's more than thirteen years ago, I realise, since I studied it in school. I had loved it then, and it had intensified my desire to see snow. The words start to return in fragments and then larger blocks.

Between the woods and frozen lake
The darkest evening of the year.

He gives his harness bells a shake
To ask if there is some mistake.
The only other sound's the sweep
Of easy wind and downy flake.

The downy flake settles itself on the intersection. I order another pot of tea and the snow continues to steadily fall as if ready now to take its time and fall forever.

For a long time I watch it. I pay the bill and walk outside. I'm wearing a Mambo beanie and a black mohair scarf. The first snowflakes I've ever felt in my life brush against my face. I have read once that there may be an invigorating, even mystical order to the haphazard profusion and variable shapes of snowflakes. Laws according to which they form. Everybody knows that no single snowflake is ever the same. So the idea of laws creating these endless differences strikes me as odd. It's the word 'laws' that doesn't fit. Snowflakes can be symmetrical but not in a Euclidian sense. They appear symmetrical but this doesn't stand up to closer inspection. Their development is irregular and fractal, and patterns of repetition appear on different scales.

I learn this from one of the books my father gave me. I will only realise retrospectively that it was his last gift to me. It is ironic to think of myself in Paris, reading his books about unstable systems as he moved inexorably towards his own chaos on Kilauea. I remember, too, that in the months before I left for Paris, he would corner me and rave on with summaries of his latest scientific readings. I imagine now that what he was doing was clinging to something concrete in order to ward off the night. And yet in the strange worlds of chaos and quantum theory that with all his great autistic love he opened up to me, the concrete is hardly the point.

I remember that one of our last conversations, the week I left for Paris, was about snowflakes.

'Signatures,' Tom had said to me that day, in one of those moments when he rambled yet was lucid enough that at least a thread could be followed. 'It's all signatures. I mean, everything leaves a signature. From evolution—fossil paleontology, divergent traits in related species, what have you—to love affairs, the damage that we carry like frowns and wrinkles on the soul.'

I said nothing, wanting to squirm in my seat but feeling it my duty to remain and listen.

'Signatures everywhere,' he continued. 'You know what I read today? Snowflakes, each one different. Think about snowflakes. Snowflakes are the records of the changing circumstances the ice encountered during its descent. At first, you think about that, I mean really contemplate it, you think that's extraordinary. You think that is simply a stunning and a beautiful fact. And in one way, it is. But then you realise, *everything* is a record of its descent through circumstances. Absolutely everything is inscribing its own story on itself. And everything is descent.'

There was a long silence. It seemed to me that a great battle was roiling inside my father, between his own understanding of his ideas and his ability to enjoy what they actually meant in the real world.

'But that, of course, makes it no less wondrous. As they fall through the atmosphere they release, you know, heat. And so that creates a charge that attracts other ice molecules.

One tip or another begins picking up molecules from the air. The incredible thing is that the whole system, the crystal, exhibits a preference to grow symmetrically in six directions at once. A microscopic preference. Not real symmetry, of course. You can't attain that, since each flight down to the ground is a different path through different events. And somewhere along the line, the thing has burst forth into a snowflake.'

'That's good, Dad. That's interesting. You tell the most beautiful stories. Tell me another one.'

'Ah, Isabelle,' he'd said then, beginning to cry, 'come here and give your old dad a hug.' He ruffled my hair as we embraced. 'I haven't been much good for you, have I?'

My face was buried in his shoulder, as it had been so often in times of joy.

'You've been fine, Dad. The best. And you'll be all right.'

I didn't believe it. I felt sick in the stomach. But I knew I had to go to Paris. There was nothing I, or Tess, or anyone, could do. Save wait, perhaps. Tess treated him with tender forbearance all this time, as if certain one day he would wake up. I held out a faint hope that the old Tom would return but in any case had some waters to traverse in my own life. Hugging him at that moment, I might well have been throwing streamers from the deck of the liner.

My father's interest in the snowflakes makes the snowflakes seem special right now as they brush across my face on Rue St Jacques. The feeling is sharper than I have imagined it would be, like tiny arrows of cold stinging my cheeks. When I hold out my hands, aware that I stand on the corner of the street as a six-year-old girl might stand in an attitude of wonder, the flakes land on my open palms but I feel no impact, however minute. No weight. It's as if the snowflakes are optical illusions, tricks of the light brought on by a winter mirage; as if they don't exist, other than for the fact that after a few seconds my hands begin to feel cold. I see snowflakes in the air but when I look at the palm of my hand there are nothing but little splinters of ice quickly melting to rivulets of water.

I walk hands in pockets to the Seine through the soft cold morning. I imagine Matt walking beside me, his arm slipped through mine. For an instant I feel myself to be a sparrow, my shallow panicked panting the best my miniature lungs can muster, my tiny heart ready to explode.

It's been more than a year and a half since he died. I yearn again for that richer love: the mutual desire, open-armed and unencumbered, for the presence of the other in our lives. Rilke said that the highest task and privilege of a relationship was 'that each should stand guard over the other's solitude.' I am getting tired now of guarding my own.

I reach the bottom of Rue St Jacques. Across the river to my right the snow is dancing in wisps and whirls around the spire of the Notre Dame cathedral, which has been cleaned after six hundred years and stands aloof like a stone ghost against the whiteness. I descend the stone stairs of the Quai de Montebello.

I wait in the small queue that has formed on the stone bank beneath the Pont au Double. The flakes of snow are pure white as they fall into the dark steel emptiness of the river; the flowing water, matte liquid, sponging up all of the day's meagre supplies of available colour and reflecting none back. At any given moment hundreds of snowflakes drop listlessly from the sky and make their tiny dimples on the surface of the water. And instantly they disappear, though the eye follows automatically in the direction of the water, expecting to see that whiteness continue. The absorption is absolute. The snowflakes fall and then are simply not there, but the river flows on regardless. *Love flows past like this flowing water.*

On the *bateau-mouche* I stand on the foredeck, protected from the snow by an eave. The complete silence of the city unnerves me. The falling snow curves towards the bow of the boat.

Up to the right the Louvre floats past. For hundreds of years the French kings and queens lived in the serene stone palace. And yet what I would like is to be relieved of the weight of history.

When eventually I arrive back at my apartment, a short boat ride back and a cold walk later, I am glad for the central heating and walk around in T-shirt and jeans. The snow continues to fall steadily, so that when I look outside I am struck with delight at its presence. I read for hours. The afternoon turns dark early and I make soup and watch weird French television and feel I am hibernating safe and secure in the softest of cocoons.

All day the snow has invigorated me and now suddenly, at nine at night, I feel a comforting exhaustion deep in my bones. I fall into bed and am asleep within minutes. I dream I am a passenger on a ship, some kind of ice-breaker. I am dropped off on the edge of Antarctica. The ship departs. There are no goodbyes. I am to spend the winter alone on a continent of ice. I am some kind of caretaker and must look after the equipment: Caterpillar tractors, generators, Nissan huts. Almost imme-diately snow begins to settle on these things and they disappear. There is a key used to unlock all the machin-ery and operate it. I plant a small flag to mark out the spot where the key is already disappearing under the snow and ice. When the ice melts in summer the key will not be hard to find.

In the dream I am alone for the whole of winter but I make a wonderful discovery. It's a freak of nature, a warm current rising up from deep in the Southern Ocean and lapping the edges of the ice continent. I find to my sur-prise and joy that it's possible to swim in a knee-to-elbow wetsuit. I wear fins and goggles and a snorkel and pass my time exploring the warm stream around the edges of the ice. Under the water is an abundance of coral and brightly coloured seaweeds and marine life. I take a video camera underwater and know that when summer comes and the icebreaker returns to pick me up I will be able to take this film back with me. The light comes through into the water, a splendid blue reflected off the shelves of overhanging ice.

In the morning I wake from the dream to a white sky and utter silence. I look out the window, my fingertips tingling with excitement, to a world of curves. Down on the street there is not a straight line in sight. I've never seen anything like it before. It is not snowing as steadily as yesterday. The air is filled with small flurries of flakes. Each flake jiggles and swirls as if connected to invisible strings.

After showering and dressing I walk out into the street and the curved world. Everything is described by circles and arcs of circles. The snow has moulded all perpendiculars into a softness I am not prepared for. The gutters are little more than undulations in whiteness between sidewalk and road. Parked cars are half hidden under bulbous blankets of snow. The thin trunks of bare trees flow gracefully to the ground, fetlocks white.

The whole world is padded. A car flows past; but other than the faint hiss of its tyres on the dirty melted snow, it makes no sound at all. The snow is a sound absorber, a vast organic muffler on the clanging of the day, each single flake soaking up the ambient noise that is afoot and that ricochets all day from source to deflected surface to ear. The air is cleaner and clearer, as if the departure of noise from the atmosphere has left a looming void in which nothing resides but hope.

I sigh. It strikes me that I have never before realised that happiness and sadness can coexist in the one body at the same time. I crouch down to a small snowdrift and pad together a snowball. My first snowball. The camera in my mind clicks. One for the family album. I stand up, snowball in hand, and quickly my hand becomes uncomfortably cold. There is no one to play with. I survey the street: pretty and white and empty. I lob the snowball like a hand grenade and in the middle of the intersection it explodes with a thud and a puff. Hands in pockets, hungry for coffee and croissant, I walk towards Le Week-End.

Volcano

AND ALL THE WHILE MY FATHER CONTINUED TO CRUMBLE away. I went so far inside my head in Paris that he disappeared somewhere near its far-distant edges; for the mind is an enormous hall, much bigger than the earth itself. I have told this story in a rambling way. I cannot help it. The wind blows through that cavernous mind and on it float fragments of aromas, half familiar, half remembered. We sniff our way back towards them but the paths are not straight. I forgot to mention that in my early months in Paris, my father had sent me a letter. It was for the most part an attempt at normal pleasantries; I imagine the enormous effort with which he fought through the Melleril and the other drugs to make his syntax work. He mentioned he'd been reading about the Jainist religion from ancient India. It never surprised me, the directions his reading took.

'What distinguishes it from all other world religions is its rigorous fatalism,' he wrote. 'The holy man Gosala, founder of an offshoot of Jainism, believed that human effort is ineffective. There is no cause, there is no motive, for the corruption of beings; beings are corrupted without cause or motive. There is no cause for the purity of beings; beings are purified without cause or motive. There is no act performed by oneself. There is no act performed by another. There is no human act. There is no force. There is no energy. There is no human vigour. There is no human courage. All living things are without will, without force, without energy. They evolve by the effort of destiny, of contingencies, of accidents, and by their own state. The Buddha, a contemporary of Gosala, thought this attitude was criminal. I'm not so sure myself. It is a curiously, attractively, neutral scheme of things—almost scientifically neutral—though a little bit frightening. For every action there's a negative reaction. So the less we act, the less negativity we cause. At any rate, sacrifice and surrender are surely the garments in which we clothe our final rest and the long repose.'

Well, that's my father's position, clearer than I can state it. Like so much else at this time, I expelled the more worrisome aspects of the letter from my mind. We are all, to a greater or lesser extent, obsessed with our more immediate surroundings, with ourselves.

One of the last clear things Tom reads before he books his ticket for Hawaii is the thing that helps to make his mind up. 'The planet Earth is essentially a slow-moving glob of liquid iron surrounded by a slightly faster-flowing layer of liquid rock on which floats a thin crust. On the margins of the ocean floor, some of that crust is being sucked into the cauldron beneath, while above, crustal plates grind into each other, spawning volcano eruptions and earthquakes: fractal and chaotic signs of the immense dynamism of the living place we inhabit. Since everywhere on Earth's thin crust the natural landscape is being hewn by chaos into shapes with branches, folds and fractures, and detail inside detail, the immense intermeshing of dynamical forces constitutes the eternal, ever changing dissonance and harmony of nature…'

He had copied the passage into the notebook he kept, a manic scrawled diary of those last weeks and days that was found in his hotel room in Waimea. A lot of it is illegible. There are long conversations with what he calls angels, and at other times, demons. These are the voices that hounded him away from the daylight world.

A lot of the rest I must piece together—though some of it is made up of facts—from onlookers and hotel staff or from Tess, and later, from the newspaper reports and from the last family to see him alive.

'I need a break,' he says to Tess. This is how it starts. 'Maybe the beach, the sun, will make a difference. You're right: all these closed curtains don't help. I have to make an effort. Nothing ambitious, nothing to worry about. I'll go to Hawaii, I'll find a hotel, find a beach, keep taking my pills, take it easy. Go for walks, a little bit of swimming. Maybe things will change soon.' He is crying now. The tears flow easily these days. 'Because this can't go on forever.'

'Oh, Tommy,' says Tess. She sits down on the arm of the chair and strokes his grey hair.

'Look at me,' he says, his eyes pleading. 'What's happened to me? What am I?'

'You're still my Ginger Meggs,' she says. 'It's a bad patch, that's all.'

'It's ten years, darl. It's more than a patch.'

She thinks of Dan, of betrayal, of prisons, and there is nothing to say to this man she loves, or loved, so much. She pulls his head to her chest and rubs the back of his neck. In the musk of her pullover it must feel to my father that toxins are flowing from his spine into his skull. He reaches his arms around her and squeezes her back. He feels nothing. Feels that he has never felt anything, and even the pain of goodbye is made small by the approach of his death. He yearns for peace.

He reads books on Mt St Helens in Washington State, on Pompeii, on Krakatau. They are spread over his desk, annotated, pored over, and remain there for weeks after his death, like a mad frieze, until Tess and I clear them away. 'You didn't see them here?' I ask her. 'They seem like such an obvious sign.'

'I haven't been in here for years,' she says. 'It was his private room. He made that clear.'

'Oh come on, Mum. What about cleaning? What, you just never came in here?'

'I never looked at his books, did I. He read all sorts of things. It was mumbo jumbo.'

'What about this?' I point to the books on the desk. 'Look at all this stuff! Look—volcanoes. Volcanoes. Look—Kilauea. Look—he's drawn arrows on this photo! How could you be so blind?'

'He could have been drawing arrows on the fucking moon, Isabelle!' Tess stands still, puffing, aggressive. 'He was going mad. *Everything* was a sign. Which signs are the important ones? You'd go mad yourself trying to keep up with that.' Crying now, bewildered, she continues to stare at me. Her shoulders heave.

'Mum—' I try to touch her. She stiffens.

'What would you have done?'

'What?'

'If you'd seen the photos? The books here. Which you couldn't have seen from Paris.'

'That's not fair, Mum. Paris was—'

'—I'm sorry.'

'I had every right to be in Paris!'

'And I didn't? Like waiting on a ghost all those years was fun? He left me years ago, you know.'

'You left him first. He wasn't *my* husband. I never betrayed him.'

It's like a slap. And then she ignores it. She lunges for the desk and rips out the page with the arrows drawn on the Kilauea photo. 'What would you have done?' She thrusts it in my face. It is all so absurd, as if my father were a famous explorer and these his final preparations. I look at the path of descent, black biro, dotted lines, arrows.

'I guess... I guess nothing. I would have let him go. I wouldn't have believed he'd kill himself like that.' With this I'm crying too, and we are holding tight to each other.

'I did betray him,' she says through her tears. 'And I wish I could have it all back. I'd go down a different path. Maybe I killed him, Isabelle.'

'Mum, you didn't kill him.'

'Maybe I killed him.'

We pack the books away. I hold on to the notebook, which the Hawaiian police had sent back to us.

In the week before he left, a murder had made the headlines. It's the fifth of the 'spinster killings': five women, all older than sixty, all living alone, all living within ten kilometres of each other in the eastern suburbs of Sydney, all dead in the last nineteen months, all hacked to death with a blunt machete, and in such a fashion—the police will not divulge details—that it is without doubt the work of one person, a serial killer, a psychopath.

Several pages of the notebook are devoted to the murders. Tom writes that he watches a feature story on TV about the hunt for the killer. The report shows file footage from the previous year, images of crime scenes sealed off with police tape, maps of the eastern suburbs spotted with arrows, police spokesmen. A British forensic psychologist, an expert in serial killings, is interviewed. 'A psychopath,' the psychologist says, 'is simply this: someone who is so wrapped up in their own pain that they are incapable of feeling, or even of being aware of, anyone else's feelings.'

I see him reaching for the remote and switching off the TV. He reaches for his pills and drinks a couple down. Then I'm no different from a murderer, he writes in his notebook. And my very presence here is a stain on the bright world.

The notebook tells me that in the toilets at Sydney Airport he throws the last of the Melleril away: new approaches for new journeys. In Hawaii he begins to drink. He embarks with glad heart on a drinking binge, one of only two or three he's ever experienced, which lasts for days. It becomes a world inverted. The notebook becomes more frenzied. There is too much light, and the journey to darkness and peace must begin. First, after a day of serious drinking, most of it on the terrace of his hotel room overlooking Waimea Bay, the angels start to arrive. They are not the familiar messengers of air and light. Rather, Tom senses them as forms, half-mongoloid, pure of intention, rising and sinking through the surface of the earth, which has become sponge-like, an intermediate zone between atmosphere and molten rock, a porous mattress of superheated moss. The walls of his hotel room throb with their presence. For a page and a half his writing is an impenetrable mass of hieroglyphics.

I imagine that the more he drinks the more the angels beckon. It is midday; too bright out there for humans with sense. Thank God for the canopy. I imagine that he is so drunk he can barely move from his chair. Fuck wha? Chair. Feel good. His legs spread out before him in a V that defines the panorama of beach. His feet push comfortably against the balcony railing so that he feels safely anchored. I picture on the black glass table beside him a bucket of ice, a can of Budweiser, a bottle of vodka three-quarters empty, a bottle of tonic water, a bowl of limes, a serrated knife. His hands are sticky with lime juice from his muddled, laughing efforts at mixing drinks. He goes inside to the shade of the room. I've led a good life I've led a good life. Have I not? he asks.

'You have,' the angels answer, their sweet innocent voices caressing his ears like a breeze in a field of lilies.

'And have done good things?'

'Yes. Have done good things.'

'I have done nothing wrong.'

'If you say so.'

'No. That's not true. It's wrong, all wrong. Half of life is wrong.'

They do not reply; the room is filled with buzzing.

Tom continues. 'Wrong to allow things to keep going like that all those years. But I felt so small. Your own brother. What would you have done? I did nothing. Wrong to suppose it could not be possible. Wrong to trust, and wrong to welcome the blindness I put on.'

'It was never blindness,' an angel says. 'You knew every-thing, always. It's hard to admit. You are only human.'

'Everything? No, not everything. There was a time when I knew nothing, nothing about it.'

'Never a time like that,' the chorus whispers, 'not so far as we know. And *we'd* know.'

'No, that's not right,' pleads Tom. 'That's just not right. I didn't know. You live in good faith. You hope for the best. You see the best in things. Assume the best. Give the benefit of the doubt.'

'Yes, when in doubt, give the benefit of the doubt.'

And then, from the other side of the hotel room, another angel, this one more sombre-voiced: 'But you were never in doubt.'

I picture my father swinging around. He is sweating a thin film of fear. He feels some disdain. 'Doubt? Doubt was all I ever knew.' He takes a long draw from the bottle of vodka. It seems to slow his heart. Then a swig of whisky: this for the hands. The angels crowd the room. 'But not doubt about that. My wife fucking my brother! Jesus...' There is a long pause. Tom hears his breathing.

'We can only repeat that you knew everything, always. Everybody always does.'

'What the fuck would you know about it? *You* know everything, maybe. Not me. Walk a mile in my shoes, you fuckers. Since when've you known what it is to be a human? I was busy trying to run my life. It's hectic, you know, doing that. I had a doctor's surgery. Sixty, seventy-hour weeks.'

'Oh, we know *all* about the surgery.'

Tom's head drops and he listens to their tittering. 'What's the point of this conversation, please?'

'No point. We're here for other reasons.'

'Right. Of course. You're here because I'm going to die. Is that it?'

'Precisely. We're here because you called upon us. We've always been here. But you called us into being. By the way, we're very appreciative of that. We don't usually get called into form. But a volcano! Such style. Sublime, in fact.'

'You're here to take me there?'

'No, you help yourself.'

'To help me do it?'

'You don't need any help.'

'You have no opinion on my death?'

'Now *that* would be truly absurd.'

'Can you offer me comfort? I'm a little drunk, I think.'

'What do you think this is, salvation? Let's strip away all mystery here. Basalt. Andesite. Dacite. Rhyolite. Silica content. Viscosity. Hard light of day. Eruptions of ash-flow plateaus. Magmatic gas. What would you prefer? Death by drowning? We could try to give you the details but it's not our particular field of expertise. Everyone knows everything, always. Everyone should stick to what they know. The mobility of the surface masks the convection currents of the deep mantle. Hot-spot volcanoes form this way. You are about to die in one. You're sitting above a deep mantle current that's three thousand miles thick and it's been circulating slowly for eighty million years. The buoyant rise of magma. Heat flux. Magma shattered by explosive boiling into lava fountains, pyroclastic fragments. Such contact with the air! What did you write on the Customs and Immigration declaration card, where it said "Purpose of Visit to the United States"? We ourselves have rejoiced at the break to routine. Your fluidised slurry awaits you, sir. Gases boiling out of the gas-rich magma. In the plate is your solace and in the mantle is your solitude. Uprush, uprush. Ah, but you want to descend. To that calm place where the blood slows down to dream. Your dreams will be ours. Tom, you won't remember yourself. Oh it is joy, joy, a day of joy. Downwind and upwind all the birds will have fled. That telltale bulge that grows along the cone slopes for weeks and months on end before the caldera collapses, before catastrophe: all this has been done for you, long ago. Earthquake swarms and flutters are absent. Magnitude 0.2. It is a peaceful day for death to come. You're in Hawaii on holidays: don't stray from your purpose. For, lo, he that formeth the mountains, and createth the wind, and declareth unto man what is his thought, that maketh the morning darkness, and treadeth upon the high places of the earth, the Lord, the God of Hosts is his name. When the groundwater heats above its subsurface boiling point it flashes into steam. Elsewhere the intruding magma is injected into the fissure. But for you we have prepared a bed of honey, since—did you read it in the brochure yet, Tom?—erupting lava has the same viscosity as honey at room temperature. The earth was incandescent four and a half billion years ago. Incandescent. Sufficiently cooled now, of course, for you to be able to decide to end it all. The slow movements in the mantle are due to the plasticity of the rock. You'll be gathered into the quicksand, beyond the hummocky deposit and the lobe that sweeps down to Spirit Lake. What is your life reduced to now but these fluidised emulsions? Nothing to be ashamed of, Thomas. We all reduce to something. On the summit the day will turn black with the ash of your weight. Then *puff!*, you are gone, the lightest of birds, so insubstantial now that your wing cannot singe even cumulus clouds. The mobile mantle rises and partially melts. In the sulphide-rich torpor we sleep. Therefore the flight shall perish from the swift and the strong shall not strengthen his force, neither shall the mighty deliver himself. The excess heat of the magma can partially melt the host rock through which it ascends. He that is swift of foot shall not deliver himself; neither shall he that rideth the horse deliver himself. Heat lowers the density of the rocks and therefore the speed of the seismic waves that travel through them. But he that is courageous among the mighty shall flee away naked in that day. And the mountains shall drop sweet wine, and all the hills shall melt. All this will be yours. For an instant.'

Tom starts to laugh. Then the laughter turns to tears. On his knees he bends to the carpet, covers his face and weeps into his cupped hands. 'I've led a good life.'

'You've led a life.'

'There was Isabelle.'

'Indeed. Your great creation.'

'Oh Bella.'

'She'll die too, Tom. You're getting off the point here.'

'The point, then. We'll stick to the point. Having said my goodbyes in my head.' He tilts the vodka bottle to his mouth and empties it. 'I got out of prison, and the architecture remained. Those ugly high walls. I remained awash in my greed.' He rolls onto his back and passes out.

Have I imagined all of this? I entered into his notebook. For a moment I reclaimed him as his mind splintered apart.

He wakes a long while later. His first thought is that his body will dry up and he fears that he will die of thirst. He staggers to the bathroom and, cupping his hands, takes a long drink of water. He pisses and then steps into the shower. I picture him sitting beneath the jet of water for half an hour, holding his head.

In the bedroom the thought occurs to him that he does not know how long he's been asleep. He picks up the phone, rings the front desk—this much we have from the hotel records—and gets straight to the point. 'What day is it, please?'

'It's Friday, sir.'

'Friday. And what time is it?'

'It's 9:15 a.m., sir.'

'Thank you very much.'

'Thank you. Have a nice day, sir.'

He's lost a whole day. As sick as he feels, he laughs.

It just isn't important, he realises, losing a day at this end of a life. I too am struck by the astonishing fact that every day we stay alive, the odds increase of our dying. There are many reasons for going on, but you could certainly be excused for not doing so.

He could continue drinking but he's been going strong now for three or four days, and there just isn't any point. He wants the Melleril, as much as possible, to be out of his system. He knows that this morning might be a small moment of clarity, might be the time to get things happening. I imagine he knows that without the Melleril, without the brakes, things might well explode, and he may never make it out of the hotel except in a hospital van.

On hotel stationery he writes a very basic will. 'Since I don't know who I love the more, I leave fifty per cent of all my possessions to my wife, Tess, and fifty per cent to my daughter, Isabelle. To my brother, Dan, I leave all the forgiveness I can muster.'

He signs it and dates it. He folds it neatly and slips it inside his passport, which he places on the pillow. He writes a letter:

Isabelle, Tess.

There is no point explaining. That would be dumb. I'm dropping downwards to the centre of things. We will meet again, in one form or another.

Your loving (and slightly crazy) husband and father,
Tom

This, too, he folds and slides inside the passport.

At the carpark beneath Mount Kilauea, where the tourists' viewing trail begins, he leaves his photo-licence propped up on the dashboard of his rental car. He scrawls a final note, to make things more obvious, and places it beside the licence. 'Passport and relevant information back at Orbis Hotel, room 314.' He locks the car and walks through the lush rainforest as the trail begins to wind its way up to the viewing area. He overtakes an American family, the children dressed in identical parkas, the father slightly overdone in shorts and long white socks and hiking boots. When later we contact them, they send us the photo they took of Tom, and an extra holiday snap of the smiling family taken halfway up the trail, Kilauea looming in the background.

Tom strides ahead. The rainforest begins to thin out and the view opens onto a barren moonscape, surreal undulations of lava spreading in all directions over acres and acres, gradually rising towards the high point a mile or so distant, from the lower southern edge of which billows smoke, lazily, as if from a country chimney. Tess and I went there five months after he died. It did not feel like a holiday. It's a brown wasteland of cracked, sere rock, the rough, broken surfaces of lava baking into basalt crinkles under the tropical sun as it inches forward year after year over the smooth, ropey surfaces of the *pahoehoe* flows. Almost home, thinks Tom. His feet are moving him forward, one in front of the other. He notes with curiosity the rhythm of their movement.

I imagine he feels he could float away now. The Melleril has gone, the alcohol has emptied out all other emotions. I imagine he feels his body beginning to fade. I imagine he imagines himself to be transparent, like a ghost in an old black and white movie. Abbott and Costello in a haunted castle. A cascade of flickering images is passing through him: the accumulated irrelevancies of a lifetime. It is high noon. There is no shadow. He sweats hard as he toils. The gradient steepens.

He registers another curious fact: the complete absence of birdcall out on this tract of Hawaiian desert. He has entered a place where nature focuses on the one thing and the one thing only: this gash in the comfort of the earth, where daylight roils in a vortex, always precariously aware of its proximity not to Night but to Under, this giant sump around which ordinary everyday nature struggles to keep its balance. This place where birds have no business.

The only sound he must be hearing is the crunch of his own shoes on the walking path, the tight puff of his breathing and, from further away, the holiday sounds of the American family. And as he comes closer to the viewing platform, he must hear the hiss of the volcano itself, which will eventually increase to a roar that will drown out all else.

He makes it to the platform an hour after he leaves the car. The American family are small specks hundreds of metres down the trail, slowly following. He leans on the railing and gains his breath. He looks at his watch. It is seven minutes past one. He thinks how this is the last time he will ever see the big hand on seven minutes and the little hand on one hour and is vaguely comforted by the thought.

The crater stretches before him like a jagged stadium, everything skewiff, everything leaning at bad angles, everything impossible to access. A geologist's nightmare. Kilauea is categorised as a shield volcano, a large dome-shaped mountain formed by countless eruptions of fluid lava over one hundred thousand years or more. The summit is indented by a cliff-walled caldera, the Halemaumau Crater, formed by inward collapse. This useless information travels in the brochure in Tom Airly's back pocket.

Far below, three hundred metres down perhaps, is the churning red maelstrom where the lava breaks through the crater. From the viewing platform it looks like a tiny red lake. I picture him putting a coin in the telescope and focusing on the lake. It bubbles and simmers, as promised, with the viscosity of liquid honey. All around, the barren moonscape hisses. The summit is rich in the carbon dioxide that leaks from the magma chamber two miles below the surface. He scans the telescope up the north cliff wall that rises from the lava lake. It's a sheer cliff of baked basalt and andesite, rising, it seems, hundreds of metres on a smooth vertical; an anomaly, a line so geometrically precise in this profusion of jaggedness. Okay then, he thinks. Final angle of descent. Looking through the telescope, trying to hold it steady, does he have a still flash of memory in which I, Isabelle, nine years old, am running around the backyard wearing welder's goggles, a white sheet attached to me as a cloak, the coathanger clasped in my hands bent to serve as the joystick of a spaceship, while I repeat in a robotic voice the immortal lines from *Star Wars*: 'Stay—on—target! Stay—on—target!'? Does he resist the urge to cry? All decisions have been made. Stay on target. The baked ash-flow plateau which leads to the cliff.

I imagine he is so calm now that he wonders his heart is even beating. He continues, with the aid of the telescope, to trace a path backwards from the final cliff, back towards where he is standing. Finally, with his naked eye, he lines up what appears to be the easiest way of descent.

He can hear the American family now, chirping away as if to make up for the absence of the birds, hidden from view behind a large boulder fifty metres away, but about to emerge around the final bend on the path. He glances at the sign erected by the local tourism authority. 'Warning: serious injury or death due to heat scalding, burns and toxic gas emissions can result beyond this barricade. It is expressly forbidden, except for members of the U.S. Geological Survey, or other authorized persons, to go beyond this point.'

He climbs over the safety barrier and lowers himself to the ground. He begins picking his way across the boulders and down towards the crater. The ugly angels have followed him all the way from the hotel. Soon they will be beautiful. They pulse all around him in the glare. He begins to hear what sounds like the hissing of steam. The day has dissipated all around him. He has moved into a giant factory, so big it can't be seen; he is no more than a molecule in one of the bolts in one of the girders, in the far corner, near the smelting chamber.

The dissonance and harmony of nature. He is comforted by the thought that as he moves across the arid terrain, his life is moving away from dissonance and towards harmony. A voice calls from behind him, 'Hello!', thirty metres back. Tom stops and turns around. It's the American father, standing with his family on the viewing platform. From this point in the story of his death, my mother and I have the American family's version of events to help piece things together. The gap between his notebook and the hard evidence is bridged.

'Are you okay there?'

'I'm sorry,' calls Tom. 'Um, I'm sorry. I just...'

'I can't hear you!' the American shouts.

Tom cups his hands over his mouth and calls louder. 'I'm fine! No problems!'

The American persists. 'But the sign here! It's dangerous out there.'

Tom laughs. 'It's dangerous everywhere!'

'What?'

'I said, I'll be all right.'

In the wasteland between their cupped hands, words are trailing and flittering like scraps of paper blown about in a vacant lot.

'But what are you doing?'

'I'm sorry about this.'

'Maybe you should come back!'

Tom smiles and shakes his head. 'Goodbye,' he calls. 'Have a nice day!' He turns and continues his descent. The American, growing alarmed, thinking in his panic he will need proof to show to the authorities, takes a photo—the one he will eventually send to Tess and me—of the tiny figure diminishing in the distance. Two days later the photograph will appear around the world in the more popular newspapers: 'Descent Into The Underworld: Final Photo Of A Suicide.'

Tom begins to follow the ledge he sighted through the telescope. The red lake is not far now. All his clothes are soaked with sweat. He strips naked, feels the heat of the ground on the soles of his feet, then puts his runners back on. He does not tie the laces. He throws his jeans and T-shirt into the canyon. He turns back to face the American family, spreads his arms and shouts to them:

'Naked!'

He looks down at the paunch of his belly, his heat-shrivelled penis. The sunlight makes his red pubic hair disappear so that he sees himself as a boy. A boy with the roar of a bull. 'Naked!' he shouts again, allowing the sound to rise up from his stomach. Then his soul seems to deflate. He tries to sit down for a minute, to gather his thoughts, but the rock is too hot for his buttocks, and it is getting hard to breathe, and his thoughts are too fast to catch. Oh God, look at me, pity me. I am an old man lost on the rocks. I am a flabby red-haired man whose life has come to nothing. I am a naked man in Reeboks, about to dive into a volcano. Please carry me downwards gently, break my fall.

In all his life Tom Airly has never spoken to God but it feels like the thing to do now.

He is finding it hard to breathe in the heat. He stops to urinate. He watches the liquid flow out for the last time ever, the gold stream glinting in the sun, the urine pooling in rivulets and gathering the dry volcanic dust into its flow before disappearing into a crevice.

The smell of hydrogen sulphide and sulphur dioxide begins to nauseate him. He forces himself to continue. He rounds a bend and looks behind him and the Americans, tiny figures, are jumping up and down and waving frantically in the distance. One of them—is it the mother?—appears to be moving away, running perhaps, back down the path, to raise the alarm.

He turns away from the last humans he will ever see. The lava lake is bubbling: huge languid swells that move out from the centre, rolling rather than breaking waves, bigger than the biggest surf he's ever seen in Sydney. From where he stands now he can see clearly the place where the ledge drops away. From that precise point there will be nothing but air and the sheerness of last things between him and great rest in the molten flow.

There is nothing but a terrifying calm surrounding him now, like silence after bells. The angels all are hushed.

He pushes one foot in front of the other. He feels that his skin is beginning to flake off in the searing heat. Five minutes, surely, and I'll be there, he says.

But he reaches a bend where the canyon wall becomes very steep and the path he is trying to keep to—or create— is barely a foothold. His Reebok slips on a scree of loose rock and his ankle twists and he loses his footing and begins to slide. There is a ledge that tilts inwards. There is space in the empty air. As his body flips over one full time the sky flashes blue across his vision. In the split second of the consciousness that he is beginning to fall, he makes the final decision of his life: not to try to grab hold of anything. *Why panic?* his brain, pulling down the security grille, says to his soul, which is already departing the store. It's the weekend; enjoy yourself. Take it easy. Have a nice day.

So I missed the centre. So? Edge or centre of the volcano, it makes no difference now. He tumbles down the slope, weightless, arms and legs flailing lazily; his neck snaps early in the fall; he comes to rest finally on a large boulder sixty-three metres below where he tripped. A small lake of red begins to form around his head.

That is everything I can possibly imagine, or deduce, or put together. All that is known for certain is this. The American family had noticed him pass them on the trail. A while later a ranger noticed the peculiar placement of his passport on the dashboard. The family became alarmed on seeing Tom climb the barrier. The strange conversation ensued; the father took the photo; the mother went back to raise the alarm and met the ranger coming up the path. By then it was too late. Tom stripped off his clothes, put his shoes back on, sat down for a moment, continued. Then apparently he just slipped on loose rock. Rescue teams reached him just before dusk. The autopsy report said he had died instantly of a broken neck. The awful phone call reached me in Paris and I was moderately drunk on an airplane when the photo was being beamed around the world. At the instant the camera clicked my father is stepping onto a small boulder, his back to the viewer, his face turned sideways, in profile. His right arm appears to be fluttering a small discreet goodbye, but he is probably only holding it out for balance.

Fish That Are Birds of the Ocean

ALL THAT SEEMS LIKE SO MUCH UNREALITY NOW. I HAVE been too much in my head. I am wrapping up the story; it has exhausted its parameters. I must try to keep it simple.

Fact: I had another funeral to get back to. But at least with my father the end was not so unexpected. I had lived with an increasingly heightened sense of the imminent arrival of tragedy in the long years as his mind unravelled. Or perhaps the madness itself was the tragedy. If there is an afterlife I assume he felt an astonished relief to be there.

At the funeral I began to cry, not so much for what

had been but for what might have been: he might have been happy. There was so much that seemed good, and so much loss. There was so much we might have shared, in the later years. In the church I was in the front pew with Mum and Uncle Dan and his family, and Dad was three feet to my left in a sealed coffin. Thirty-six inches is not very far in the scheme of things. My chest constricted and I thought it might burst. It is absolutely necessary to believe that the soul has left the body, because the concept of claustrophobia is untenable. I imagined him at rest somewhere, and regret assailed me: he had been going away from us all, for a very long time. Could I have done something to bring him back? I began to weep then; it all poured out. I wept through most of the service and into the afternoon. Mum held my hand, Dan patted me on the back. I wept all night; I cried myself to sleep. He would sit with me in the backyard. I orchestrated tea-parties, for just the two of us. I invented characters for him and he slipped obediently into his role. As the sun set on warm spring evenings and Tess cooked dinner, his patience was infinite. We played hide-and-seek. He really tried hard to hide. After the funeral I wept for weeks. On the edge of athletics fields all over Sydney, he stood and watched me stretching, sprinting, jumping. He stayed long evenings at training: not in the car, not reading a book, but standing, watching me. I glowed in the gaze of his love. From across the lanes of the running track and the sandpit of the long jump, through the jumble of sports bags and equipment, he applauded me, politely, reverently. At the aquarium he held my hand and we admired the stingrays and sharks. In 1978, with the utmost grace and never a complaint, he took me to see *Star Wars* at least five times. At the funeral it was apparent that he was utterly gone from us. I wept for weeks. He was only fifty-six.

As for the survivors: it was a horrendous blur, Tom's funeral and the emptiness of the aftermath, the endlessly sorrowful months that followed. During this time I grew closer to my mother than ever before. In the stream of my love I let go of mad Tom Airly and away he floated; I welcomed into myself more easily the memories of Tom the red-haired god.

Morbid though my trip to Hawaii with Tess might have been, it was a catharsis of sorts. We booked into the same hotel as Tom. We shopped and went swimming as if in a dream. On the fourth day we went up to the volcano. In sweltering heat under a viscous grey sky we sat on a flat rock and looked out over the baked lava plain. Wisps of smoke seeped from hidden fissures. I tried to imagine him clambering up the path and over the safety railing.

'There was something pure about his determination,' I said.

Tess said: 'He must have been like a child that day. A little boy.'

The tension was gone. We spoke for hours. Tess opened up her life for me more fully than any other time. She talked of everything, of her own childhood, of Constance, of the early years with Tom. Of Dan. Finally we got around to the affair.

'It wasn't—it wasn't planned. It wasn't like I thought, Hello, this is a good idea.'

'Doesn't matter, Mum. Maybe Dad would still be with us.'

'We'll never know that. What happened up here could be genetic. It could be anything.'

'But you kept going. I can understand how something can just…happen. But you kept *going*. Didn't you think there was a right and wrong?'

She sighed. 'Right and wrong. Of course I did. Of course I did.'

'And…?'

'And…and all the other shades as well.'

'What shades?'

'You know—right and wrong and all the shades between. It confuses me today as much as it did then. I was younger than you are. Do *you* feel old?'

'I still feel eighteen. I always feel eighteen.'

'And so did I. When you feel like that, it's like you can do anything. I adored them both. I only loved your father. But time stood still when I was with Dan.'

'You mean it went fast with Tom?'

'I'm fifty-three,' she said. 'You know how old I feel?'

'How old?'

'Fifty-three. And you know what I want?'

I shrugged.

'Two things right now. I want to tell you I'm sorry…'

She reached out, held my hand. '... And I want you to forgive me.'

I looked at her, no longer young, not really old, and loved her. Despite it all.

Paris is over for the time being. Tom is over, Matt long gone. When Tom dies I take that curve through air again, back around the globe to Sydney and to ocean. I return to Australia, to the diamond light and the sense of space. I still have some of Matt's insurance money left.

Heaven is in the heart and hell is in the head. If you don't take notice of the obvious signs then it's no surprise when you lose your way. Some time after Dad's funeral I go to Byron Bay for a week or two, to clear my head, to see what it's like up there these days, to learn how to scuba dive. Why not? There's an underside to every surface. At Byron Bay there are wild storms. For two whole days and nights the waves are six metres high and television news crews come from Sydney and Brisbane: good visuals. The waves strike the storm barrier at Main Beach and wash over the carpark where once, years earlier, in the summer holidays from art college, I had eaten fish and chips and laughed with Louise. The tourists are pissed off. The surfers, too: the sea has gone beyond 'awesome', beyond 'bitching', and is now too dangerous to surf. All through the grey days, groups of people gather on the headlands, wrapped in ineffectual windcheaters and buffeted by the colossal winds, to watch the churning ocean, so astonishingly violent. On

Cape Byron the air howls with the boom and screech of breakers smashing on the rocks below.

In a loud cafe I sip coffee and write a postcard to Tess.

Dear Mum

Wild weather, bucketing down. Byron Bay wrapped in a gale for three days—cloud ceiling about ten metres; streets awash, gutters running out of control, trees whip-whipping and out the window the sea gone mad—giant white rollers in slo-mo heaving landward from a mile out. Pretty exciting. Hope you are well.

Love Isabelle

'Calamity!' the local paper trumpets, in a cover story about the summer tourist dollar lost. I am enlivened by the happy calamity of the weather. On the second night, as the gale reaches its peak, I walk the twenty minutes to Main Beach from the bungalow I'm renting—a ramshackle hippy weatherboard belonging to a friend of a friend. Cosy in my hooded sweatshirt, I sit in a barbecue shelter out of the main force of the wind and watch the scene, the night seething with salt spume. The high street-lights on their space-age metal stilts clatter backwards and forwards, like masts on a ketch about to disintegrate, over the slick deck that is the deserted carpark. The air is thick with white ocean foam, blown in all directions at once. It's as if a snowstorm has descended on the asphalt carpark and is held there swirling by conflicting gravitational fields. I blow into my cupped hands and imagine in there a peaceful place. After half an hour I go back to the bungalow and curl up in bed. Beneath the sheets is a tiny world of comfort, far from where the wind howls, in which I feel solace. I know the house to be secure, though the wind causes the tin roof to sing.

In the morning I open my eyes to silence. Expecting noise, I am not even sure I am awake. I lift myself on one elbow to gaze out the window. Clouds are moving fast, like caravels with sails unfurled, across a crisp sky. The windowpane, the eaves, the plants and shrubs in the garden, are shimmering and expectant with droplets of water, and every drop seems an extravagance. The world quivers in the greenness. A magpie struts across the yard.

Good, I think, throwing the blankets aside. Diving soon.

Though the weather now is fine, the sea takes another three days to unchurn itself, and then suddenly it is laid-back heaven in Byron, the way the brochures depict it.

I enrol at the Deep Six Dive School and promptly fall in lust, though only temporarily, with Charlie, the instructor, who resembles Willem Dafoe. I read the dive book studiously at night and practise all the manoeuvres during the day. On the third day of classes, when Charlie asks me what I'm doing later, I think he's taken about twenty-four hours too long. I am happy all the same. I touch him several times on the arm at dinner that night while assailing him with the chronologically incoherent, high-speed intensity of my life story as we meander our slick-fingered way through a lobster feast, trying to let him know that, yes, it would be good to fuck tonight. Yes, I'm only here temporarily and yes, please pick up the signals and let us not waste time. When he walks me home to my door and only leans forward to kiss me once on the cheek, I listen to the voice of my blood and take pity on his boyishness—he is only twenty-three—and clasp the nape of his neck in my hand and lead his mouth mine. Charlie is surprised, but not so surprised as to not continue.

We kiss and fuck all night. The needle arm of the turntable is faulty—there is a CD player but the old vinyl collection is better—so that when a record ends the needle lifts and returns to the start. Thus we hear, this night, a crackly side one of Tim Buckley's *Greetings from L.A.* perhaps fifteen times. It is like dream music to our liquid callisthenics.

Four days later I receive my laminated certificate and card: Open Water Diver. I've done two preliminary pool dives, a beach entry, and four boat dives, including a wreck.

Afterwards Charlie takes me aside. 'It's my day off tomorrow, and I can get the second boat. I'm going to take you somewhere special.'

'Great! Where?'

'It's the Minnow Bluff. We don't take schools there, because there are some dangerous currents and we'd get into legal trouble if anyone got hurt. But privately it's okay.

Not as part of the school. It's where that American guy on his honeymoon got taken by a great white last year. But don't worry, that was a freak accident, very unusual.'

'Very unusual. Well, that's a relief then.'

'No, I'm serious. It'll be okay,' he continues. 'It's beautiful there. It's the right time of year. It's a surprise. It's a present for you. You wait till you see it.'

In the morning we leave just after sunrise, walking sleepy-headed from the bungalow to the dive shop's storeroom, loading the boat with our wetsuits and tanks and heading out to sea to Charlie's secret spot. I am reminded of good times with Matt. I feel older, but lighter. We track the coast for twenty minutes and then veer east, towards a horizon that divides two different shades of blue.

We come upon a submerged reef two kilometres offshore, a safe anchorage only on relatively calm days, for an hour or two during high tide. Charlie weighs anchor from both stern and bow, just to be safe, and we help each other with our tanks and equipment. We jump from the boat into the water.

'You okay?' asks Charlie.

I've already put on my mouthpiece and mask. I raise my thumb and nod.

'Let's do it then,' he says, and we go under.

Visibility is extraordinary, at least twenty-five metres, as if the storm has never occurred. We descend nine metres to the plateau of the reef and glide around the rocks and luminous vegetation as fish eye us with cautious curiosity.

We are levitating on the top of an underwater mountain. Charlie motions to follow, and disappears over the edge.

With two kicks of my fins I too reach the edge of the precipice and allow myself to fall downwards. I feel I am an eagle, wings outstretched, held aloft by the wind and slowly descending a sheer cliff face. Halfway down the cliff I pass a moray eel loitering in a crevice, its ugly head bobbing backwards and forwards in the attitude of an imbecile, its mouth opening and closing as if chewing its cud or locked in an eternal effort to utter some fact for which words do not exist.

By regulating my buoyancy control device I can reascend and drop slightly so that gradually I trace a zigzagging perpendicular down towards the ledge where Charlie waits at a depth of twenty metres. He is partly obscured by a slow-motion whirlwind of tropical fish. When he waves at me the fish go into a temporary flurry and for a moment he is clearly visible, hovering upright, his fins keeping balance on the small sandy floor of the ledge. Then the fish reassemble themselves into the thick swirls of colour that hover near his webbing sack of breadcrumbs.

He passes the sack to me. I feed the fish hesitantly at first, my hand jerking back involuntarily as the bolder among them lunge for the bread and peck my fingers. There are fish everywhere. My eyes meet Charlie's. It is strange to be in a situation of such unexpected and intense pleasure and yet physically not be able to laugh.

When the bread is finished Charlie beckons me to follow again. We round the corner from the ledge and come into a verdant valley, a luxurious V-shaped depression in the reef where fish of every variety dart and foliage sways and a strong current can be felt tugging from the dark blue distance.

For fifteen minutes I explore the valley, all my senses exquisitely attuned to the thrill of this freedom of movement through three-dimensional space. Perhaps it is like my dream. Perhaps I am leaving that Antarctic ledge behind, and down here, deeper than I expected, are the warm currents.

A large groper follows me wherever I go, colourless and bland among the psychedelic fauna, almost human in the expression of stress and seriousness it wears on its face. I imagine it saying to me, 'I don't belong here. I'm made for better things. Please get me out.'

I am busy peering into a fissure and watching some strange crustacean either mating with or killing one of its own when Charlie taps me on the shoulder. I turn around and he points upwards. I look towards the surface. I almost gasp and take in water; it is all I can do to keep breathing into my mouthpiece.

Above our heads is passing an immense flock of stingrays. There are hundreds of them, in orderly formation, like a flotilla, the lowest only a few metres above us. It is a staggering sight, such a strange and determined convoy passing through the valley. But the most extraordinary thing is that, without exception, their wings are all moving with exactly the same motion.

There is only one single thing in the world, in the history of my entire life, that I can compare the situation to. It's the convoys of spaceships, the allied forces gathering to destroy the evil Death Star, lumbering through the depths of space in my second-favourite movie of all time (after *Star Wars,* of course), *The Empire Strikes Back.*

The ranks pass above us, langorous and graceful, six or seven abreast and several layers high, so that light is blocked out. Their wings seem to ripple in translucent silhouettes. I move an arm up towards the lowest ranks above me and merely cause a gentle undulation in the flow of movement.

When the last of the stingrays has passed overhead, the light that filters down through the water reformulates itself. The sun's rays reach down through the water like slats of liquid light, to illuminate the coloured fish, the coral, the seaweed that sways at the bottom of the valley. But it's time to begin the return, punctuated by rest-points to avoid decompression sickness, to that world from where we departed twenty minutes earlier.

So this is Charlie's gift. I know it will remain one of the best presents I've ever received in my life. Charlie will be gone soon—he's a handsome boy and a good fuck but not a lasting proposition—yet this thing here, these moments in the Minnow Bluff, will move into my blood and lodge there forever. Everything there for the taking in.

What appears to be chance is in actual fact providence. When the fin kicks down here, or the crossbar quivers on the high-jump, then providence moves too. At any rate, chance favours the hungry mind, the open posture. Chance occurs, as Laura the captain said, when we become prepared for it.

We ascend five metres and follow the stingrays for a minute, tailing the tail-enders. It's like joining a flock of migrating pterodactyls, in an imaginary age four hundred million years earlier, on a planet where the atmosphere flows like honey. We kick forward and move through the flock for a while, swooping and gliding among the huge rays. The stingrays take not the slightest notice of us, only altering their trajectories slightly to avoid making contact with these alien creatures. Then Charlie and I stop, and hover, fins moving softly in that weightlessness, and the flock recedes into the gloom.

At the surface we rip off our masks.

'Fuck! Fuck! How was that?' shouts Charlie.

'That was...that was...' I can barely speak for laughing. 'That was incredible, Charlie. That was unbelievable.'

On the deck of the boat, stripping down from my wetsuit, I say, 'But how often do they come here? How did you know they'd be there at that moment?'

'I didn't.' Charlie laughs. 'I had no idea!'

'You're kidding me.'

'I had no idea in the wide world, Isabelle. I swear. The

present, I mean the special treat, was just the Bluff itself, the valley filled with fish. That would have been enough. I've never even seen *two* giant stingray together, let alone anything like that. It wasn't me, baby. I thought it must have been you. I knew you were special but I didn't know you put on shows like that!'

I laugh. 'But where were they going? What were they doing?'

'I have no idea,' says Charlie. He is full of life, generous and keen, and I hope his own future brings him bounty.

That night I pack my bag. Ten days' worth of dirty clothes, and the handful of books I brought along. Charlie comes over later and we make love one last time. In the morning we swap addresses and phone numbers, more out of a sense of social habit than the knowledge that we will ever look at them again. Everyone moves so much, anyway, that numbers are never valid for more than a year.

'Look me up if you're in Sydney,' I say. 'I might be back up here next year. I'll do the same.'

But I know that words are empty in this phase of my life. Conversation is weightless. Filled with light, it can pleasantly infuse the hours. There is the absence of Matt, which means that his body is gone, and all his words are unspoken now and will be that way always. Likewise my lonely father, drifting at peace somewhere else in the heavy slumber of forever. But something is rumbling towards me from the future. Isabelle's Glorious Precept Number One: I am subject to the delivery schedules of timetables not my own. I look forward to the time when I will inhabit my own body again and enter conversations at the moment they actually occur. To the uncertain and ambiguous gods in whom I partially believe, I pray for patience.

POSTSCRIPT

 *2006*

THAT WAS MATT'S DEATH AND DAD'S DEATH. THERE are details afterwards that don't need to be told here. A lot happens in six years. Life pans out. Now, at thirty-six, I am giving birth to my second child. A boy is about to arrive. The first, a girl, Morgan, is already two years old, flame-haired and pale-skinned like me.

The room in the birthing centre is sterile, pleasant, all creams and yellows and some sunlight leaking through the vertical blinds. But I prefer to spend as much time as possible in the adjoining room, with its large spa and shower. While Morgan's birth was an ordeal, I am relaxed, excited even, about this one: I know more of what to expect. I have slept from nine last night to five this morning, when my waters broke. I arrived at the hospital at 7 a.m. and at eight-thirty I am less than an hour away from giving birth. Michael has just returned, having first dropped me at the hospital and then taken Morgan to Tess's to be babysat.

He fishes; he's a fisherman, operating charter boats. He lectures a little too. We met six years ago, not long after Dad died. I was thirty; he was forty, emerging from a marriage that had drifted into decay. He was lecturing in the marine coxswain's course that I'd started taking soon after I got back from Byron Bay.

One night the class—eleven men, of whom two or three were morons, plus me, who nobody quite knew how to take—was learning about 'Marine Survival.' We went out to the Qantas emergency simulation training terminal. I had to jump from a ten-metre height, fully dressed and in a life jacket, and drag other members of the class to safety. I had to right a flipped life raft, help the others in, then climb aboard myself during a simulated storm, in darkness, while being sprayed by fire hoses. Once we were all huddled on the raft, one of the men started telling an obscene joke about a woman. Being the only woman on the raft, I didn't take kindly to his lack of tact.

What's apparent is that life is very short and there are times when a gentle acceptance will just not do. Sometimes, taking a stand doesn't do anyone any harm. I punched him in the face with all my might. It was not part of my normal nature and had I known how much a punch would hurt my fist, I would never have done it. It was a circumstance beyond my control. As he teetered backwards in shock and pain, I launched my foot into his chest, hard into the logo on his life jacket, to help the momentum along.

In the darkness Michael, supervising events from the side of the mock-ocean, heard a shout, a commotion, then a splash. It was Michael, my future husband, who had to gather together the different versions of events and decide on a course of action. The joker was threatening to press charges for assault. The general consensus was that he had it coming. The one thing Michael wasn't prepared for was to fall in love with his student, me. In my written explanation of events, as lucid, as concise and as strongly argued as I could manage, I acknowledged the inappropriateness of my actions and apologised for the disruption to the class. On a separate sheet of paper I wrote, for the joker:

> I apologise for punching you in the nose and kicking you off the life raft during the simulated storm.
>
> I. Airly

Michael deemed it wise to throw the amusing but possibly inflammatory letter into the bin. (As for the joker, he came up eventually with the face-saving opinion that 'The bitch was probably on the rag; let's just let it drop.') Curious for more contact, Michael responded to my letter, thanking me for my explanation and implying that, unofficially, he admired what I had done. I wrote back to

Michael, to thank him for his lectures and teaching, and to explain more, off the record, about how I had felt that night and why I had done what I did. I had intended the letter to be short but found myself rambling in unexpected directions.

'Ultimately,' I wrote, 'I think that your biggest fear is that because you are a woman, in the end you might always be vulnerable. Because the average man sucks. I guess that's why I love the sea. It makes me feel strong. You know what you are dealing with. It's a force that is stronger than anything, any man or woman.'

It was common ground, or ocean, enough. Enough for his heart to move a fraction. Enough for him to phone me—inappropriate use of the school database, as I love to remind him—not knowing even if I was in or out of a relationship. 'This might sound dumb,' he said, 'but I was wondering if you'd like to meet for a drink some evening.'

A couple of years later we were married. It was a nice event, very low-key, a small church; Louise, my beautiful bridesmaid bedecked with flowers. Uncle Dan, big cheesy grin, the family man, the Futon King, gave me away. It's a funny old world. Maybe I should hate him the most. For that moment of transgression, which started everything. But hatred has a way of feeding on itself. Hatred means having someone living rent-free inside your head. If the past, like the future, gets too big in there, then the present can be a very narrow place. On the other hand it seems the more we manage to live in the moment, the more infinite it becomes.

And now here I am. Now comes our second child. The spa bath stands in the middle of the white-tiled room. From the wall protrudes a detachable sci-fi shower nozzle. Stainless-steel handles are bolted to the wall on either side of the shower. Between contractions I use the handles to lower or raise myself. Sitting in the spa, I am soothed by jets of warm water. I drop my head forward and play the nozzle over my neck and upper back. Michael, sitting in his Speedos on the side of the spa, moves forward to take the nozzle from me and spray my back.

'No, no more,' I say, panting.

'Do you want me to rub your back?' he asks.

'No, nothing right now,' I say. 'I can't be touched right now.'

I slump delirious beneath the spray of water. I know that even between the closest couples infinite distances continue to exist. The trick we seem to be trying to discover lies in how to love this distance. Then there is the greater chance that each can see the other from head to toe. And there he is, Michael—God bless his kind soul—on the edge of the spa. You make a choice and a thousand events spring forth from it.

I stand up under the jet of water. I lean my hands against the wall and my head droops, languidly, in the onset of pain as the water cascades over me and another contraction begins. Then a great strength wells up in me, beginning as a tingle in my feet. I feel uncomfortable and turn, reach out to either side of me and clasp the handles so that now

I am standing in the position of crucifixion. I arch my head upwards, then roll it around my shoulders, feeling the luxuriant strain on the muscles in my neck. I push my chest forward, leaning outwards from the metal grips.

I start to hallucinate. In less than a second a new world opens out and I am somewhere richer than any dream. I am the figurehead of a ship slicing its way through a vast ocean, heaving and indigo and ink blue and emerald green. My head tilts back into the onrush of wind. The spray of the shower is the salt spray whipped up from the incision that the prow makes and borne aloft on the currents of air. I am the figurehead, carving through that world; the me giving birth knows the pleasure of being transported for an instant from pain. Swordfish are speeding through the water, silver streaks keeping pace with the ship. They leap from the whitewash, powerful arcs. Holding onto the handles I lean forward as far as I can balance, lean into the speed and the beauty of it all, and breathe deeply the wild salt air. From behind me I hear the rustle and flap of the great canvas sails being hammered by the wind. Soon, helped by the midwife and Michael, I will move out of the spa and onto the bed in the birthing room next door, and Thomas will be born. But for now I move forward on an endless sea, at the prow of a ship. At sea there is always a horizon, beyond which can be anything.

Acknowledgments

MANY THANKS FOR MANY REASONS.

For accommodation and hospitality during a period of flux and a great deal of travel—
In Sydney: Steven Betts for Hall Street and, more importantly, friendship; Nick Trevallion; Andy Harding and Louise Bell; Marty, Gisele, Adele and Mark; Chris Noonan and Glenys Rowe for the greatest apartment in the universe, on the Ben Buckler cliffs; Mum; Jane Gleeson-White. On the NSW North Coast: Jane Healy; Jane Simpson and John Habib and family; Uncle Pat; Anne and John Simpson; Cassie, Jan and Luke at the Bales. In Paris: Suzie Longbottom; Franck Michel; Janet Christea; George Hayim; Rupert and Charlotte Ball-Greene; Nathalie Rafal; Chloe Fox. In Dublin: Michael West and Annie Ryan.

Acknowledgments

In London: Guy Halliday; and the wonderful Geraldine Aron. In the USA: David Hackworthy for New York, and his generosity and friendship; Dan Hennessy for Los Angeles; Albert, Lisa and Maria Sulprizio for Los Angeles. In Spain: Lluis and Cesca Llobet at the Centre d'Art i Natura in the Pyrenées. Elsewhere: Shelley Perkins, for the Marriott connection, and for being a friend.

Regarding the book itself—
My thanks to the Literature Fund of the Australia Council, in conjunction with the Australian Ireland Fund, for a three-month Writer's Residency at the Tyrone Guthrie Centre for the Arts at Annaghmakerrig, County Monaghan. And to the Literature Fund, in conjunction with Insearch UTS, formerly known as Insearch Language Centre, at the University of Technology, Sydney, for the Writers in Asia Partnership Program which awarded me a three-month residency in northern Thailand. Particular thanks to Michael Fay, former Director of Insearch, for his dedication, support and belief in the Program. And to Andrew Coyle of the Australian Centre in Chiang Mai, for his generosity and kindness.

Some of Tom's strange ramblings about science draw upon information found in *Fractals: the Patterns of Chaos* by John Briggs, from which comes the 'dissonance and harmony of nature' quote in the chapter 'Volcano.' In the same chapter, the 'holy man Gosala' passage draws upon the Samannaphala Sutta 54 as paraphrased in Eliade's *History of World Religions*.

Thank you for kind permission to reproduce part of 'Stopping by the Woods on a Snowy Evening' (p. 203) from *The Poetry of Robert Frost* edited by Edward Connery Lathem copyright

1923, © 1969 by Henry Holt and Co., copyright 1951 by Robert Frost. Reprinted by permission of Henry Holt and Company, LLC.

The prose translation of the Apollinaire poem 'Sous le Pont Mirabeau' (p. 158) is the author's.

Special thanks to all those involved at close range as the drafts progressed: Jane Gleeson-White (once again), my agents Gaby Naher at Jill Hickson Associates and Fiona Inglis at Curtis Brown, and to Sophie Cunningham, Christa Munns and Annette Barlow at my publishers Allen & Unwin. To Breeze Delian. To my editor Sandy Webster, for her sublime skills and her uncanny ability to find the thin novel trapped inside the fat novel's body.

To Gisele Menge and Bernard Cohen, for patiently listening in Paris to my reading aloud of the first chapters—now happily non-existent—I ever wrote for this book. And for being polite, I guess. To Mille Jensen for listening, in Chiang Rai, to the chapter 'Love Calls You by Your Name,' which *does* still exist.

To Darren Wensor of the Little Athletics Association of NSW, for information about believable high-jump records for nine-year-olds.

To the great people at Dashing Printing in Bondi Junction—may we continue to do good business for years to come.

To John P ('Jack') Lockwood, volcanologist extraordinaire, of Hawaii, who kindly checked the chapter 'Volcano' for basic technical details. (And check him out at <www.volcanologist.com>.)

To Bobbie McDonald, whose story of Marine Island inspired young Isabelle's version in the chapter 'Meat Truck.'

To Graham and Lynley Rayner for helping me with crayfishing and Abrolhos Island details in Geraldton, Western

Acknowledgments

Australia. To Deborah Robertson for Fremantle, and the road trip. To Jimmy and Bronte Younger for the house in Kalbarri, and to Jimmy for his patience with my sea-sickness (an illness to which Isabelle, of course, never succumbs!) the day we went out from Geraldton.

To Etgar Keret, wonderful writer and true genius, for allowing me to use his 'algorithm of wandering' idea in the chapter 'Birds That Are Fish of the Sky.'

To Dr Robert Muller and Dr Geoffrey Bradshaw for help with some medical and psychiatric details regarding Tom Airly.

To Dr Paul Payne, astronomer extraordinaire, of the Sydney Observatory, for explaining the scattering of blue light by air molecules.

To Julia Leigh for reminding me of the great Barry Lopez quote used at the beginning of Part Two.

To Sister Jenny Neilsen, of Royal North Shore Hospital in Sydney, for explaining—in more detail than I probably wanted!—the possible physical effects on the body of impact with a moving truck.

To Sophie Russell in Paris, for telling me a strange story that somehow morphed its way into 'Zooming.'

To Sarah, who first told me about hallucinating while giving birth.

To Dad.

To Jeremy Fitzgerald, who set the example, walks the walk.

And to Christina Alves, ship's captain, of Lisbon, some of whose strength and beauty is in this book.